RUNNING FOR HOPE

YOUNG SCHOLAR AUTHORS

Anaia Brewster
Zakar Campbell
Kennedi Carter
Summayah El-Azzioui
Ayah Eltayeb
Nya Furtick
Jordan Griffith-Simmon
Arthur Harrell
Jordan Jarmon
Zabria Justice
Mini Kpa

Maritza Mercado
Claire Morris-Benedict
Layla Musawwir
Ryan Odom
Macey Owen
Brianna Pinto
Dacia Redmond
Matteo Rios
Alma Rostagni
Olivia Rostagni
Izzy Salazar

Mira Sanderson
Eden Segbefia
H'Be Siu
Ned Swansey
Khari Talley
Khori Talley
Antonio Taylor
Zoe Tallmadge
Kobie Williams
La'Zayrea Smith
Qua'Sean Williams

ADVISORS

Barbara Blue
Doug Coleman
Katie Fernelius

Alexa Garvoille
J. Lorand Matory
David Stein

RUNNING FOR HOPE

JOHN HOPE FRANKLIN
YOUNG SCHOLARS

EDITORS

ALEXA GARVOILLE
DAVID STEIN

The short text excerpts captured in the graphic illustrations are from *Mirror to America, The Autobiography of John Hope Franklin*. They are found on pages 10, 51, 93, 120, 129, and 159. © 2005 by John Hope Franklin and published by Farrar, Straus and Giroux.

Visit us on the web! http://jhfyoungscholars.tumblr.com

Illustrations by L. Jamal Walton, Malcolm Goff, and Delvecchio Faison
Back cover photographs by Jenny Warburg

ISBN 13   978-1-5055-0233-6
ISBN 10   1-5055-0233-0

Kendrick Parker isn't quite sure what's going on with his life. He doesn't know if the girl he is interested in really likes him back and his best friend is having troubles of her own. More importantly, his parents are keeping him up at night with their yelling. It's getting harder and harder to get to school on time, something his history and track coach, Mr. Douglass notices. Hoping to inspire Kendrick, Mr. Douglass hands him a copy of the graphic novel version of *Mirror to America*, renowned historian John Hope Franklin's autobiography. Little does he realize how much it will encourage him to take action.

PREFACE

The keys to the holding cells in the courthouse were enormous, great chunks of iron that appeared to have been handmade. I saw them in the North Carolina mountains, while doing a final edit of this book, after I came across a description of a holding cell where our main character finds himself. The jail passage was written by one of our thirty John Hope Franklin Young Scholars.

I was skeptical big clunky keys were still used in 2009 when our story is set. So I drove into Marion, North Carolina, and asked if I could see a holding cell they would have used in that period. The student's description turned out to be very accurate.

I was surprised one of our sixth through ninth grade Young Scholars would have known in such detail what a holding cell looked like. I shouldn't have been. These remarkable students poured themselves and their research skills into this book.

We began the summer with a simple idea: to learn as much about the remarkable historian, John Hope Franklin, as we could, and then write a book about him for Young Adults. To make it more engaging, one of out scholars, Izzy Salazar, suggested a hybrid book similar to Brian Selznick's *Wonderstruck*. We were sold—it would be two stories wrapped in one. The first component was John Hope's autobiography in illustrated form. The second was that of ninth grader Kendrick Parker, who is going through some tough times.

One of our first challenges was coming up with a way for Kendrick to get in trouble. Led by Duke student Katie Fernelius, the group brainstormed all the ways kids get into trouble in school. It was eye-opening as they recounted what they had seen or done themselves. From the long list, the Young Scholars voted on what should be included in the book. The adults nixed the most popular one, a true story of a student (not one of ours) defecating in a school's bathroom sink. So the group selected the second one instead: the knife. It seemed both outrageous and accurate.

When I mentioned the book project at the Wildacres Writing Retreat in July 2014, the assembled authors were skeptical of how thirty young teens could collaborate successfully on a book. What they didn't see was our own writer's retreats, the character development using life-sized figures they built and carried around, the dialogues between characters captured with iPhones, and the guidance we received from outstanding writers like National Book Award winner Phillip Hoose, detective author Katie Munger, workshop leader Zelda Lockhart, and the historical fiction author, Sharon Ewell Foster, who won many awards for her Nat Turner books. They also never met Alexa Garvoille, a remarkable English teacher at Durham School of the Arts, who had already published four books with her students and provided the steady hand throughout the whole process.

# # #

The Young Scholars also engaged with John Hope Franklin's world. We traveled to Orchid Trails Greenhouse to learn about orchids, one of John Hope's passions, and to each take care of our own. John Hope also loved fly-fishing, so we practiced with Jim Coveney and friends in the middle of Duke's West Campus quad.

Fortunately John Hope's papers are at Duke University and the library staff brought out boxes and boxes for the Young Scholars to read through. They found he wrote supportive letters to almost everyone who wrote to him; received large royalty checks for his groundbreaking text, *From Slavery to Freedom*; loved his wife passionately; and received significantly more honorary degrees than any other person in the world. We were astonished he didn't seem to have any enemies, and even won over the woman who called him a "Harvard nigger." Yet this was also a man who spoke his mind with elegance, courage, and humor.

Though the young man of our story gets into far more trouble and steps outside the bounds of what John Hope would ever have considered doing, we hope you will see elements of him in Kendrick and will feel inspired by both.

Therefore, we invite you to journey into the life of a young teen's struggles and successes through his unexpected interactions with John Hope Franklin.

David Stein

PART ONE

– 1 –

I forced my bare feet into some Jordans and pulled a black beanie over my cropped waves. Standing up straight, I examined myself in the mirror. I was barely fifteen, but I had grown four inches over the summer. Now I had to stoop to fit my six-foot frame into the mirror above my dresser. But when I looked, I saw that my chin jutted out too far and my eyes peered from under a too-strong brow. I flashed myself a winning smile as I flexed a bicep and winked.

"Kendrick Parker," I said to myself, loud enough to relish the new depth in my voice but not wake my dad. "You, sir, are looking especially fine this morning after only 2.4 hours of sleep. You are assuredly the most handsome and intelligent and—" I couldn't help laughing at how ridiculous I looked. "—full-of-crap boy."

I unlatched my bedroom window and hauled it open. It screeched a little, and I stopped, listening for any early morning movements below. The silent morning breeze rummaged around my messy room, flipping humid fingers through the pages of a book I'd left open on my bed.

After wedging myself through the open window, I stepped gingerly onto the roof, still damp with dew. I'd been climbing out my bedroom window for years, but now it was a lot more difficult than it was when I was nine.

I squinted in the direction of Lia's house and could just barely see the second story bedroom light on. I contemplated texting her, then dropped the thought. She'd probably fallen asleep reading again. Lia had been my best friend since the fourth grade when she moved to Durham for her mom's job at Duke. She had grown up on the knee of a grad student, so her mother's dissertation on Richard Wright was the closest thing she could remember to bedtime stories. I'd say not many other young children were wrapped in literature around racial themes, particularly documenting the suffering of African Americans after the Civil War. That's part of what made her special. But this morning, her house seemed strangely far, so instead I looked up to watch the wisps of clouds move over the even-more distant moon. I sat for a moment on the windowsill, listening. And thinking about being alone.

I was up now because I couldn't do anything else besides lie awake in bed imagining worst-case scenarios. Last night was the worst it had been between them. I was in my room, half attempting to do math, half listening to my parents, and half being annoyed at my hair. Yeah, I know you can't have three halves, but that's basically how well I was able to do my homework at that point. My parents had been "talking" most of the evening, which explains the 2.4 hours of sleep.

It would start as a normal conversation, about who would take the cat or whether the books she gave him for his birthday were his or hers if he didn't actually want them. Then the sound would grow from beneath the floorboards like a monster under my bed and I'd have to turn up my music louder just to pretend I wasn't listening because for some reason this was the worst thing that had ever happened to me.

And then it'd be quiet.

And then I'd wonder what they were doing. Staring laser beams at each other?

And then I'd start my own conversation: *Who would I live with? Would Mom still like me when I was at Dad's? What if I became a pawn between them?*

Well, it was quiet now because Mom had decided to tiptoe right out of the house and drive off to my Aunt Charlene's over in Woodcroft, a neighborhood about twenty minutes from where I grew up in Trinity Park. She had woken me around three to tell me she was leaving for the night, that it was best for her, and that dad would take me to school. I pretended to be asleep when she came in, and I pretended not to cry when she left.

Now, I felt the morning air on my skin. The humidity clung to me, but it wouldn't for long. Fall was coming in more ways than one.

I took another look at the moon. "I've gotta get out of here, too," I said and stood up on the slate roof.

But I wasn't running away. Not like Mom did last night. I was just running because that's one thing I knew how to do well.

Yes, I wanted to run so fast that I'd leave my own body in the dust. My blood, half mom and half dad, was now a mixture at war and it would never keep up. I thought, maybe, if I ran faster than light, faster than heredity, faster than the year it takes between separation and divorce, maybe I could find the future without having to live through the present. I could be the Invisible Man, a colorless specter—but I'd never get away from myself.

In fact, when you're running, you are the only constant: your thoughts are your rhythm. Everything else speeds by, but you remain the same. So Coach Douglass' Zen teachings had started to take root, after all.

I carefully descended from the second-story roof to the pergola before jumping down to land on the pink gravel that crunched like ice under my feet. After about a week of sneaking out to avoid my parents' fights, I had learned to do it quietly. My feet kicked up the little pebbles as my legs took me away.

- 2 -

The ride to school that morning was awkward, to say the least. Dad was tired and emotional, and I didn't know what to say. So I just looked ahead, watching the trees and houses roll by until he'd pulled up into the drop-off lane. I climbed out of the car, and told him I loved him in a voice I'm not sure he even heard.

I spent the first part of the day half-asleep, zoning out in Algebra, Earth Science, and Spanish. But when I got to fourth period with Mr. Douglass, I snapped out of my haze. I loved World History, plus, Douglass was my cross country coach, so we already had something good going on.

There was no sign marking the room, just a number—107—and only those in my class knew how welcoming that number truly was. Inside, it seemed like the kind of place you might find a slam poet spitting flow about black power. The walls were decorated with ancient-looking posters of Dr. King, Harvey Milk, and John Hope Franklin—who looked strangely familiar. I felt myself drift back into time. Was it four years ago?

I remember sitting between my parents, tilting my head back so it hit the sharp edge of my white plastic chair. We were just three rows back, so I could clearly see the black and white photographs of authors layered on the wall next to the podium. Standing up there was a familiar face from

4

a book cover. Yes! I remembered it all now. We were downstairs in the Regulator Bookshop on Ninth Street, listening to John Hope Franklin read from his just-published autobiography, *Mirror to America*. This was back when everything was good, and my parents took me to book signings weekly, all over the city, any type of author, reading from books on any topic. On this particular day, Dr. Franklin spoke of his upbringing in Oklahoma, and then later, researching in the State Department Archives and History in Raleigh, pushing his cart through the stacks, which were

I remembered walking up to the table where he had sat after the reading, clutching his heavy life in my hands. He shook my hand, gazing kindly at me through large wire rimmed glasses, exactly as he did on the cover of the book I struggled to keep in my sweaty grasp. He asked my name, which he carefully wrote out on the title page, and signed his name underneath. I still have the book on one of my shelves. I'd never read the whole thing, often getting through the first few pages and then having to put it down and run off to find a dictionary. I made a mental note to myself to look for it and try again when I got home.

Back to present day now, Kendrick, I reminded myself. I glanced at the wall to the right of me. A construction paper mosaic on one of the tattered bulletin boards depicted the March on Washington in a faded rainbow of geometric shapes.

We sat about in chipped, one-piece wooden desks, trading observations with our friends as Mr. Douglass, dressed in his thrift-store elbow-patch jacket, paced the room with wild eyes. As much as I appreciated Mr. Douglass as a teacher, I couldn't say much about his sense of style. I swear he only had two pairs of shoes, four pairs of pants, and a collection of about eight shirts. And the socks were always black. At least he rotated his collection so he didn't wear the same thing two days in a row.

I was curious enough about his background that I Googled him. It's not stalking—he just never talked about his own history, which created space for us, his students, to make up quite a colorful one. I found out he used to work as an administrator at Duke in the history department. Before that he had taught in a Harambee School near Kisumu, Kenya. And he attended both Antioch College and UC Berkeley, so he had to be a real leftie.

I don't think I was the only one drawn to Mr. Douglass. I think the others appreciated how unpredictable he was—like playing Tom Lehrer songs to teach about civil rights. The kids on cross-country liked him, too. The other day he challenged us to jump in the air and click our feet together twice. Which we tried, of course, only to discover it was a lot harder than we thought. "It's all about rhythm," Mr. Douglass said, and had us clap out a beat. Then we jumped and it was easier to do the double-click. "Running is all about rhythm, too," he continued, and we practiced running and clapping at the same time.

Today, a passage from John Hope Franklin's book *From Slavery to Freedom* was projected on the screen. The lights were dimmed in reverential respect. In the background, Pete Seeger strummed his five-string banjo and sang about not being afraid.

The bell rang and Douglass walked to the front of the classroom. "I'm going to take a break from what we've been talking about this week, and switch over to something I *personally* would like the entire human population to know about—"

"Starving children in Africa?" Some snickers escaped from the rows behind me and I turned to see the source of the comment. I wasn't *trying* to do the whole old-man-glaring-at-kids-in-the-movie-theater routine, but I couldn't help but activate my laser eyes and go all teacher-face as Oliver slouched into his desk and fist-bumped the kid sitting next to him. Douglass ignored them. He was a pro.

Today, Oliver matched his signature bow tie with a deep green button-down tucked into his belted skinny khakis. His long legs, always crossed in class like some pseudo-intellectual, were shorn in colorful trouser socks: forest green herringbone against electric blue. He would rock his crossed foot during discussions, meditatively, as if his waxed Clarks were slowly intimidating his opponents. His eyes, dark against creamy skin, would glance furtively around the room as if to ask, 'Who's next?'

"I want to talk about the Wilmington Massacre of 1898. If you'll remember, I gave you a reading assignment about it for homework on Friday to get you ready for today. Would you please get that out now?"

I grinned at my paper. Now *this* was a subject I knew about. After reading the paper on it, I had gotten down every book in Dad's library that ever mentioned the one and only successful coup d'état in the U.S.A. Lia had even loaned me her mom's copy of *The Marrow of Tradition*, which was sitting open on my bed now. It covered the same territory as a book my dad had shown me, *A Day of Blood* by LeRae Umfleet. Dad said he got it when he went to the tribute marking the one hundredth anniversary of the massacre. I bet Lia's mom had been there, too.

"Now, can anyone tell me why I'm calling this event a 'Massacre' and not a 'Race Riot'? Kendrick, perhaps?" said Mr. Douglass, straightening the sleeves of his faded sports jacket with the charcoal grey patches.

"You're calling it a Massacre because the African Americans involved were unarmed, while the whites were, *and* more than twenty blacks were shot, but not a single white man was harmed. Also, the term 'Race Riot' tends to make people think that it was race against race, full out and bloody."

"Precisely, Kendrick, thank you—although, it actually *was* 'full out and bloody,' as you say," said Mr. Douglass, giving me a rare smile. "Now, some of you may have noticed I said this was an event I *personally* want the human race to know about." His eyes held a moment on the back corner of the room. "This is because it is not in the state curriculum. In fact, most people don't hear about the Wilmington Massacre until they're in college—or not even then! For homework, due Friday, I want each of you to write two paragraphs on why you think it's not in the curriculum, and why not many people know about it. Remember: there is not necessarily one right or wrong answer. That's why I'm giving you four days to think about it."

Mr. Douglass had gotten so worked up that he was now striding back and forth across the classroom, spinning slightly on the toes of his One-Stars each time he turned.

If all teachers were this excited about what they taught, then the world would most definitely be a better place, I thought to myself, the files in my brain already brimming with ideas to write my two paragraphs tonight. *I wonder if he'll accept two pages?*

Is it because the oppressors write history? And they want to keep the embarrassing parts away from young, independent-thinking students? Could I maybe tie in a bit of Winston Churchill's quote about how the winners are always the ones who write the histories—

"Kendrick? Can you tell me why Alexander Manly was such a noteworthy figure?"

Oops. I had let my mind wander too far away and had missed another ten minutes of the real world.

"Um, because he was the editor of the only black-owned newspaper in the South? And possibly the only black-owned daily paper in the whole country?"

"Correct. Follow-up question: what about Manly made him generally disliked by white people?"

This one I knew immediately. "His father was white and his mother was black—and he had written some rather controversial editorials in the newspaper."

As the words of praise came out of Mr. Douglass' mouth, I felt as if I were on cloud nine. It had been a long time since I had heard encouraging words from someone other than my mother.

I wish he could be my teacher for all of high school, I thought, sighing to myself. I was only in ninth grade, so I'd have plenty of time to soak in all the Douglass wisdom.

Mr. Douglass gave the class a written assignment to work on—something that was actually in the curriculum—when he was done lecturing for the day. When I had finished, I looked around to see everyone else still working.

Kelsey sat a few rows behind me, and when I leaned back in my desk to peek at her paper, I saw she was still on her first sentence. Kelsey was slender and pretty with bright green eyes and long, light brown hair. You couldn't help but notice her. Her eyelashes were delicate, and her smile made her face practically glow. She dressed in tight jeans and shirts from top brands like Forever 22, or whatever that store's called. I'd known her since sixth grade, but the most I'd ever said to her outside of class was "Hey." Even though she was popular, she was also kind, independent, and smart. Usually, she didn't seem to know or care that she was a whole social group above me.

So in case you didn't realize, at the time I was pretty sure she was perfect in every way.

And also in case you didn't realize, she was way out of my league. Now, maybe I'd watched too many movies, but I wanted the exact opposite of what my parents had. No fighting, no arguments. I wanted the opposite. That's all I needed.

This is my time, I thought. I was going to do it. I was going to make my move.

Leaning back I whispered across the rows, "Hey—"

Yeah, good start, man.

She looked up at me.

"—Do you need any help? Because I'm alr-"

"I'm fine, I can do this by myself," she responded in clipped tones before flashing a smile so quick I wasn't even sure it happened.

Slumping back in my seat, my heart raced. *Why did I do that? She hates me now.* I felt like had I insulted her intelligence. I saw a few people look up, noticing our awkward encounter. They were probably astonished that I would deign to insult the perfect Kelsey Buchanan. A little embarrassed, I pretended to make corrections on my paper.

The class was silent, everyone hard at work, so it was difficult not to notice Oliver get up and walk towards Kelsey. *What could he possibly be doing?* I asked myself. I wanted to see the encounter clearly, so I casually got up to sharpen my perfectly sharp pencil. I overheard Oliver whispering to Kelsey, "Hey, do you need any help?"

"Yeah, sure."

I couldn't believe it!

Oliver Martin had always been the classiest dude in school; when he transferred in the middle of seventh grade, he was an instant hit. And he still was.

Maybe it was because of his style. For instance, now, as he leaned toward Kelsey, I inspected Oliver's bow tie—this one had anchors on it, little white ones that danced in different directions on a navy blue field. I looked down at my bright white Jordans and adjusted my t-shirt. The bow tie was his "in" with the administration, a team of men who for some reason came together over this bygone accessory. They brought it back. There was even a Bow-Tie Club. And Oliver was its poster child.

Or maybe it was because his light skin made it possible for him to be friends with everyone without it being a big deal. He was more Vanilla Wafer than Oreo, and for some reason that got him in with the girls especially, who were already fanning themselves over John Legend and Drake. And if we're talking the cookie metaphors here, I was a chocolate Double-Stuft Oreo dipped in chocolate milk. . .

I sat in my seat staring at my paper. *Why? Why was it that when I offered her help I was insulting her intelligence and when he offered it he was being 'sweet'?* Three minutes until class ended, and I could hear Kelsey giggling in the back of the classroom.

I'm falling for a girl who likes jerks. Great.

When the bell rang at the end of fourth period, I dashed out of the classroom, glancing back briefly to see Oliver still helping Kelsey, their heads bent over the textbook. She was blushing. I headed towards lunch, eyebrows furrowed.

- 3 -

scanned the long cafeteria tables for a welcoming face to brighten my dampened mood. Finally, through the forest of people, I spotted Lia sitting at the table in the farthest corner of the room. I let a relieved grin crack my rock hard expression. Finally, someone I could depend on to be their usual, steadfast self. Lia would always be Lia, and we'd always be there for each other.

It was me who had brought Lia back to the living when her mom died from breast cancer two years earlier. It was me who made her laugh and invited her over for dinner when her dad went in a deep depression that we would only learn later was alcoholism. It was also me who listened to her rants about Jessica, the woman her dad married only one year after her mother's death—a woman who was young enough to be Lia's sister and was artificial in every way possible. Her long extensions, her sickly sweet voice, and her plastic boobs that Lia's dad had gotten for her as a birthday present all pointed to the one truth about her: she was a fraud.

Lia now wasn't the same Lia I had known when we first met before her mom passed, but I was glad to see that she still had the same comforting air to her. It was evident now as she greeted me when I sat down next to her.

"Kendrick, I am so glad to see you! You won't believe this fact I learned in science class. So, there was this genetic study of people who self-identified as African Americans, but what they found was that the percentage of Western African genes ranged in the subjects from ninety-nine percent all the way down to one percent, which totally brings into question the validity of creating genetically specific medicines and treatments targeted towards those of African descent . . . " Yes, *this* is Lia.

Lia wore acid-washed jeans tucked into hot pink, patent-leather Docs and she always accessorized with a book—today it was *Native Son* by Richard Wright, the margins scrawled with her mother's unintelligible handwriting. "Listen to this section my mom underlined," said Lia, when she saw me eyeing the book. "'They hate because they fear, and they fear because they feel that the deepest feelings of their lives are being assaulted and outraged.'"

"That is some heavy stuff," I said. "Let me see." I thumbed through the pages and came to another underlined section. I read out loud, "'Men can starve from a lack of self-realization as much as they can from a lack of bread.' Preach. Right now I feel like I'm starving from both, though," I tried to joke. "Your mother must have been quite a radical when she was younger." Lia blushed and smiled, her large, almond-shaped eyes widening.

It was moments like these when I couldn't believe that the little girl in fourth grade with the braids had turned into this. She still had a smooth complexion, but now she wore her hair natural, sporting thick corkscrew curls that bounced when she walked or turned her head. Her wardrobe consisted almost entirely of thrift shop t-shirts bearing inspirational messages or prints. She would tell people it was her way of carrying on someone else's legacy of happiness. Oliver always thought she was crazy to wear someone else's clothes. "You don't know where that's been," he'd said in eighth grade, suggesting that maybe she'd fished it from out of the toilet. But what else would you expect from him?

Today's shirt, surprisingly, read *Hollister* in bold white textured letters. Even if it was from the thrift shop, personally I thought all it shouted was *Look at How Mainstream I Am.*

"Kendrick? Kendrick!" Lia said snapping me back to reality. She looked behind her. "Were you looking at *Kel*-sey?" she said in a sing-songy voice. "Let me go talk to her for you!"

"No! Shh! Stop it, Lia."

That was the one fault I found with my best friend—she could never let me deal with girls myself. I mean, sometimes it's good to have a wingman, but I just wasn't up for it. Not today.

As Oliver walked by, his chest probably swelling by the second from his previous encounter with Kelsey, he slid right beside Lia at our table, putting his arm around her shoulder immediately. He took all the gusto and artificial confidence he could have possibly mustered at that moment, and released it in the worst possible way.

"Aw, that's sweet babe, but you didn't have to dress up to get my attention," he said with conviction, looking her up and down. Oliver spit those words as if Lia was the mic and he was the horrible rapper trying to freestyle to an audience who wouldn't listen worth a dime. Lia raised her eyebrows at me and smirked before looking back at Oliver. He made a kissing sound in the air and then moved on.

"Bye!" she called after him, teasing.

"Don't encourage him! Even if you're joking, don't." *That slime-ball of false flirts and kiss-ups is public enemy number one,* I thought. All that I could do was hope Lia wouldn't fall for his short childish antics and would stay away from his phony new change of interest in girls. Lia would never be interested in him, and I wanted to be there to make him realize he was knocking on the wrong door. I mean, that wasn't Lia—she wasn't for the whole charismatic act he was trying to pull.

That day, I decided to leave Oliver alone because I had always recognized that in some ways we were similar. We were both smart. Both fast runners. We had actually been friends—close friends—for about six months of seventh grade. But now that we were in high school, something had changed. At one point, he dropped me altogether. I'd heard it was at the encouragement of some of his other friends.

We were also both looking for something, but looking for it in different ways. Apparently Oliver was looking for it in friends and girls—he was popular and always had been. But I was a loner, except for Lia, of course. I guess I didn't know where to look for what I was looking for.

What was I looking for again? I wasn't even sure what I had anymore. I guess men *can* starve from a lack of self-realization.

# # #

After school that day, Mr. Douglass caught me in the hall to make sure I was coming to the cross-country meeting. But at that point, I was already thinking about walking over to Dad's office and another awkward car ride and an empty house and texting Mom again to make sure she was okay.

I just nodded my response to Coach, letting him know I'd be there, but he caught me by the arm before I could continue. "Hey, Kendrick—hold up a sec. You got a minute?"

I nodded again and Mr. Douglass walked into his classroom. "Is everything okay? Something going on at home?" I didn't know how teachers knew this stuff, or if he had psychic powers, but the way he looked at me convinced me it was okay.

"Yeah, just more difficulties between Mom and Dad right now. Plus—I guess—just some girl drama. High school stuff." I tried to brush it off. Douglass had been leaning against a desk and he nodded, tight-lipped for a beat, before springing up. He paced to the back of the room and ran his fingers over the spines of some of his books, before pulling off a thin volume. It looked like a comic.

"You're so bright. And you have a lot to say. Keep your head in the game. Here." He handed me the book. "I just got this in the mail—just came out, special order. A graphic novelization of *Mirror to America*. I think you'll enjoy it." I took it in my hands and started flipping through the pages. "Dr. Franklin was once fifteen, too, you know? You'll make it through. And you're going to have an impact. I can tell. Keep your head in the game."

"Dad!"

The exhaust fan whirred like a jet engine to nowhere. My dad had been weird ever since the separation papers had been finalized a few weeks ago. This morning he was especially out of sorts.

Mom said they had to live "separate and apart" for a year before they could get divorced. Apparently, this was starting. Something made me think it was her idea. They'd talked about it a few weeks ago, but nothing had happened. Mom didn't even leave until last night, and even then it didn't seem planned, what with the three a.m. departure. I wondered if the divorce would even really happen. Lia said her parents once almost got divorced but then didn't go through with it. I suppose that's when her mom first got sick.

It was weird. I'd always thought my parents were perfect for each other: two nerdy workaholics who actually laughed at the other's jokes. Then I hit middle school. That's when Dad got his promotion and spent most of his time at work or golfing with work buddies. Mom would help me with my homework and cook dinner. It was great. I mean, it was *fine*. But now there was this. I often thought back to when we first had "the talk." It was at the end of a summer full of change, now about a month ago. I had always expected my parents to be together forever.

When they had called me into the living room that August evening, they'd looked at each other and then at me. After a moment, my father sighed. "What's going on?" I'd said. "Did someone die in the family? Tell me please, you guys are worrying me."

My dad looked at me and said, "Son, you know your mom and I have been together for a long time, right?"

I replied quickly, "Yes?"

My dad took another big sigh. "Listen, there comes a time when parents have to decide what's best for the relationship."

I started to worry even more what was going on. "Wait. What are you saying, Dad?"

"After twenty long years of being married, we have decided now we—just can't make it work anymore," my father said hesitantly.

"No. This can't be happening. What's wrong? Let me help. What is it?"

Nothing but silence filled the room. I flopped onto the loveseat across from them in disbelief. I looked around the living room I had grown up in, imagining half of the books, half of the pictures, half of the furniture, half of my family—gone.

My mother interrupted the sound of the whirring air conditioner and the cutting of the ceiling fan with her soothing voice. "Kendrick, your father and I love you very much. We will all be happier this way. It'll be hard at first, but this is what we need." She looked me in the eyes and held me there. My mom was still wearing her scrubs, and even with tears in her eyes, she was radiant. That evening, she wore oversized pearl earrings, and her hair was twisted into a braided bun.

Tears now welled in my eyes—I couldn't help following my mother's lead. "But Mom, we can fix this."

My dad stepped in. "Son, sometimes people grow apart. And that's okay. Your mother and I just aren't the same people we were when we got married."

Another wave of silence filled the room. I tried to imagine them twenty years ago. All I could call up was the wedding pictures in the hallway, pictures that now seemed to be a lie.

"This is not your fault, Kendrick, and I don't want you walking around thinking that it is—because it's not. Your father and I are going our separate ways now, and it will be best for you and this family if we just—get a divorce."

I sat there in disbelief; I couldn't say a word. All I could focus on was the bad taste in my mouth. My parents used to always be happy around each other, and they were so full of life.

But I began to remember sometime in eighth grade when it started to go downhill. They were arguing more and yelling at each other, and sometimes at me. Later they started to argue every day, then twice a day. Something told me they were going to get divorce, but I had removed that thought from my brain because I didn't want to believe it. I thought they would have fixed it by the time I turned fourteen, but it didn't work. One day over the summer, I heard them threaten each other and they almost fought. If it wasn't for me being there, yelling at them from the sidelines, it could have gotten out of control. And now here we were. Having "the talk."

That night was so emotional for me; I didn't know what to do. I didn't know how I would start high school with all that on my plate. "It's going to be okay, Kendrick," my mom had said to me as she held me in her arms. The rest of the summer had involved quiet arrangements, some loud arguments, a few tears, and my mom's migration into the guest bedroom. That was more than a month ago. But last night was only the second time she didn't stay under our roof.

When I walked into the kitchen at 6:45 this morning, Dad was wearing one of Mom's aprons, holding a brown egg in his right hand, and staring into the lights under the oven hood. *Good*, I thought. *He's making breakfast. We can do this.*

I sat there in disbelief; I couldn't say a word.

"Morning, Dad."

He started talking, too, but soon I realized he wasn't talking to me. Nor was he making breakfast, though he sure was trying. I just stood in the doorway, stock-still, and listened.

"What does that even mean, 'When I'm here I'm not here?'" He seemed to be asking the air in front of the stove.

17

"Dad?"

"Who paid your med school tuition? Who picked up our son from school every day during your residency? And what, pray tell, does he have that's worth throwing away twenty years of marriage?"

"Dad!"

I gave up on him. That morning, I would quietly grab a lunch and walk to school.

- 5 -

"Dang, Kendrick, you hadda bring the entire kitchen, didn't you?"

The cafeteria smelled, once again, like a skunk had died inside of it and decomposed, so I was happy I had brought my own lunch—packed by yours truly—even if it meant my friend Shawn made fun of me. Lia was doing some math tutoring during lunch today, which meant I got to sit with him.

Shawn called himself a Fallacious Freshman, his own ninth-grade version of Super Senior, which he would surely be. He was short for his age, which made us a strange pair: tall, gangly black dude and short little white kid palling around together. Shawn wore his mousy brown hair buzzed and was beginning to grow the wisps of a mustache. His dark brown eyes, part skeptical, part scared, constantly surveyed his surroundings, but as far as I knew, he was scared of nothing. And this is why I liked Shawn: by association, he made me feel emboldened and alive. We got into debates on all sorts of topics—politics, religion, war, education, you name it. Even though he was technically a failure in school, Shawn was a genius. Shawn didn't ever do homework, as a matter of principle, but he read Proudhon and Emma Goldman, and when he was feeling lazy, novels like *The Monkey Wrench Gang* and *Zen and the Art of Motorcycle*

Maintenance. He was an anarchist, and you could tell by the way he acted in class, constantly interrupting the teacher and telling his classmates what to think. I mean, that and the "A" in a circle he had scrawled onto his binder with White-Out that now rested between us on the cafeteria table. Wait, he had a binder?! Shawn was always surprising me. Sure, I knew he was a "bad influence," but I liked the kind of intellectual challenge he could offer me. Who else could talk to me about how dress code was a conspiracy theory and locker searches were a violation of personal property rights?

So I untied the Harris Teeter plastic bag and took out the "entire kitchen," as he called it: half a loaf of honey wheat bread, a jar of crunchy peanut butter, a jar of jelly, and a butter knife.

Ms. Curnitt suddenly turned around to see the source of Shawn's exclamation. Just as I'd screwed open the jar of peanut butter, ready to plunge the knife in, she began to speed-walk toward our table.

She frowned at me. "What are you doing with a knife in school?"

"Um, making a sandwich?"

"You know what the school policy is on violent weapons."

Shawn and I looked at each other, wide-eyed. "Conspiracy," Shawn whispered behind a cupped hand.

She was now standing over me with an outstretched arm and an open palm. I stuttered, trying to once again explain the obvious reason for having a butter knife at lunch. Did knife + peanut butter + jelly + loaf of bread ≠ peanut butter and jelly sandwich? Would Lia need to come and explain the math to *her*?

She pretended to insist on listening to what I had to say, giving me one of those 'Go ahead and try to defend yourself young man' looks, but words were no longer coming out of my mouth. She took the knife from my hand and said, "Get. Up. Now."

It was then that Principal Reynolds, wearing an oversized red and blue striped bow tie, walked by on his rounds. Ms. Curnitt called him over to inform him of my being armed and dangerous. He took the knife. I watched the exchange, wondering if I was dreaming. I was still hungry.

"Come with me, you – you – " he stuttered trying to find a word that was insulting but not insulting enough to get him in trouble. I still didn't know this administration well, and clearly they didn't know me, so I found myself being pulled toward the main office, as if by the ear.

I walked a few steps behind the principal, looking everywhere except in front of me. I saw a whole bulletin board of anti-bullying signs and thought, *What if the school is bullying me?*

Turning the corner between the cafeteria's side entrance and the foreign language hallway, I saw Oliver walking toward me. "Good afternoon, Mr. Reynolds," he quipped, standing tall and flashing his yellow hall pass.

"Mr. Martin. Nice bow tie."

As he passed, he looked at my lunch bag, all jars and bread, now dangling from my clenched fist. "Lunch in a plastic Harris Teeter bag? Nice touch, Young Money. Verrrry classy."

I arrived in the office and took a seat in front of Mr. Reynolds' desk. I felt scared going in there just because the color of my sins.

It was like every other principal's office: a huge wooden desk taking up half the room, leather chairs placed at every corner, and a placard saying *Welcome* even though the students knew they were not.

It was just a butter knife, I thought. Never did I imagine that this would cause so much controversy. "I was just making lunch. I mean, it wasn't like I was gonna hurt anyone." Confused, I had no idea what to say next.

"Look young man, I don't know what your problem is, but I just have an itch of suspicion that you're behind some of the other situations that have come up over this first month of school. You don't think I see you because you are always quiet and polite, but I can see right through your little act," fired Mr. Reynolds.

"But sir, I—"

"No if, ands, or buts about it. You have been causing too much trouble and have been making this school a worse place for other kids. We're going to be calling your father and getting him to pick you up now. This is going to be an immediate ten-day suspension with a recommendation for long-term." I had no idea what "trouble" he was talking about. Was it really me he was thinking of?

"Mr. Reynolds, I just needed something to eat on the go. My mom wasn't there to make my lunch. I didn't mean to hurt anyone," I responded, acting as if I had already committed some unseemly crime. I sat uneasily in my chair, shifting from left to right.

Mr. Reynolds saw this immediately and I could tell he thought that I was lying about not wanting to hurt anyone. He called my father and sent me out in the waiting area. There, I contemplated dipping my finger into the peanut butter, and whether I could roll up a piece of bread tightly enough to make a dipper for the jelly. But I decided this wouldn't help my case.

Dad was there after only about ten minutes, being that he worked just down the street at NC Mutual. The school secretary called into Reynolds' office, and he invited the two of us in again. The office was silent for a beat. My father stared me down as if someone had committed an unsolved crime.

After explaining the situation again, the principal continued, "Mr. Parker—"

"You can call me Buck," my father interjected, trying to be friendly. My dad looked like a linebacker and his name was Buck—how could you mess with that?

"—*Mr.* Parker, I don't think Kendrick understands the consequences of his actions."

My father, speechless, didn't know whether to bark at me and agree with the principal or call attention to the reality that it was just a butter knife.

Dad finally spoke up. He looked me up and down, and with a different tone of voice he said, "I'm disappointed in you, Kendrick."

Not knowing what to say or do, I just leaned back in the leather seat, tilting my head until I could feel the wooden edging of the chair against my neck. I briefly examined the ceiling.

Most words that authority figures say tend to blast by us, because we know the truth about what happened. But when someone tells you they're 'disappointed in you,' it just makes telling the truth feel useless.

"Mr. Parker, Kendrick is being suspended immediately from school," the principal said calmly.

"I understand." My father smiled, shook hands with Mr. Reynolds, and we left.

At least I'd gotten to go to history already. Dad and I walked down the halls in silence. All for what? A butter knife.

Just then, the bell rang, and the hallways suddenly flooded with students. Everyone was looking at me, accompanied by my father. They swerved around us, staring. I ducked my head, trying to hide my face, feeling ashamed and not like myself, my plastic bag still in hand. I stopped for a second as my father walked ahead, oblivious. When his head was just visible above the sea of students, I jogged to catch up.

As we walked to the car, I heard him mumble something about having to miss work. When we each buckled in, Dad asked me, "How did you really get in trouble? What did you do?"

"I brought a *butter knife* to school," I replied. "For my *lunch*. For peanut *butter*."

My father shook his head, clearly preparing himself for his mountain-out-of-a-molehill routine. "You can't keep doing stuff like this to yourself. It doesn't help that you dress like a hoodlum, but it's even worse that you get in trouble, too. Probably that Shawn character you've been hanging around with has put these thoughts in your head—"

"Wait, these are hoodlum clothes?" I asked, pulling on my Nike t-shirt and running pants. "This is a shirt and pants. And you and Mom bought them!" My voice was getting louder. The seatbelt chafed close against my now-thumping chest.

"Plus, I only brought a quote unquote knife to school because I was trying to pack my own lunch, like a man, since you drove Mom out of the house. Oh, and while we're on the subject, maybe you didn't notice that I walked to school while you were busy crying to yourself in the kitchen."

now looked out the window at the afternoon bustle, offensively bright against the confusion of the day. Dead silence filled the car as it bumped over potholes.

"You know what, I should just stop trying to help you because obviously you are a hopeless case," Dad seethed. I shook my head and smiled in disbelief. I was almost proud of him. Finally trying to parent me after so many years of letting Mom take the lead. It was on.

"If I'm such a hopeless case, why don't you let me go live with Mom since you obviously think she's a hopeless case, too? Yeah, that sounds perfect, we can be hopeless together!" I shouted, ignoring the sting of the words Dad had said about me being hopeless. I could see the tears welling up in Dad's eyes again, though they remained focused on the road.

I thought that maybe if I ignored and rebelled against my father, Dad would call Mom to discipline me and she would come back. Or maybe I was still in shock about how butter knives were now being classified as violent weapons. I heard the engine accelerate as my father's eyes fixed on the road. I gripped the armrest on the door and my stomach grumbled.

And then I heard the sirens. I jumped in my seat and turned around.

"You've gotta be kidding me," I heard my dad say under his breath, as he quickly wiped the corners of his eyes. He blinked, then looked calmly in the rearview mirror and slowed down, pulling onto the side of the road and clicking on his hazards.

"You always keep your hands on the steering wheel. Be polite."

As the police officer came to the car, my dad signaled for me to be silent. I nodded as he put down the window.

"License and registration," a pair of sunglasses said, leaning over the car. The police officer looked young, with short buzzed hair and a splatter of freckles across his nose. I could see myself in his glasses. I quickly looked away, afraid he might sense I had just been suspended.

"Good afternoon, Officer," my father said as pleasantly as he could manage and reached over to open the glove compartment, which fell open to hit my knees. It was the same voice he'd used with Reynolds.

"Nice car," the man said, leaning in to look at the interior. I soon realized that the man's eyes seemed to inspect my father, perhaps searching for signs of nervousness, looking for sweat or an accelerated pulse. What if I'd made him so upset that the officer now thought he was suspicious? He did start to sweat whenever he got upset. But he seemed to have things under control. I wondered, though, if the officer noticed how completely freaked out I was.

"Thank you," my dad said, handing the documents to the officer. That's when I saw the handcuffs. The officer stood up again to briefly inspect the papers and look out at traffic roaring by beside us. Then I saw the gun.

Somehow it scared me just looking at it. I thought back to some of the local news stories I'd heard earlier this year, about traffic stops leading to violence, about racial slurs coming from the mouths of the police. I wondered for a moment if 1898 was nearer than I had thought. But then, what was this cop thinking? Did he think we were thugs? Black men in a fancy car? I mean, it *was* a 2005 BMW M3 convertible. Dad didn't like to put the top down, though. A motorcycle sped by my dad's open window, and I looked at the gun again.

The officer now leaned down and looked right at me.

"Why isn't he in school?"

I could feel my ears start to flush. My heart pounded through my brain, and all I could imagine now was my mug shot on the front page of The Slammer, one of those cheap papers that prints the pictures of newly minted jailbirds.

"Dentist's appointment."

The officer nodded. "Wait here a moment."

As he sauntered back to his vehicle, handcuffs clanging, I turned to my dad, full of nerves. "Bet he's gonna issue you a DWB: driving while black." My father just looked at me. "I mean, either that or you're harboring an armed criminal. Oh, no, wait, they confiscated my butter knife in school. I mean, your butter knife."

"Kendrick."

"Wait, do I have a dentist's appointment?"

"Kendrick."

I'd heard Dad talk about being pulled over before. It's not even that he was speeding. Or was he? Maybe he just had a nice car. And he had a nice car because he worked long hours at the office instead of spending quality time with his son. Or his wife. Or maybe we were just on the wrong street at the wrong time.

He just curved his strong hands over the steering wheel and said, "Kendrick Hope Parker, this world is not perfect. You will have to work harder and be better than everyone else. That's how you'll find success. That's how I found mine."

"But I—"

My father shot me a glance as the officer reappeared.

"Do you have any guns or drugs in the vehicle?"

"No, sir." My father appeared calm.

I almost asked whether a jar of peanut butter could be classified as a gun, but I could tell this was getting serious. "Do you mind if I have a look?"

"No, sir."

"Thank you for your cooperation. Could you step out of the car, please?" My father unbuckled his seatbelt and got out. The man used his flashlight to look around the driver's seat.

"What is it you're looking for?"

"Routine search of a suspicious vehicle. Got a call about a black BMW headed this direction," he replied. Slowly, my dad looked up to the sky, probably thinking a silent prayer. The policeman noticed him doing this. "Can you open the trunk, sir?" he asked. With jaw clenched, my father reached his hand into his pocket to push the button on his set of keys. The trunk slowly opened without his even looking.

I watched on, in awe of my father's calm composure. I looked at him now with a new sense of respect. He had

You have to follow the rules to the different worlds at different times—*and* stay true to who you are.

always seemed so stiff with his conservative suits, muted ties, and solid color shirts. The thin mustache on his lip was like from another generation. And even when he was not working, which was not very often, he was dressed immaculately. Now I saw why he acted and dressed this way. I had a feeling this was his armor to deal with tough situations like this.

I wondered if the police officer had a warrant or if there was another reason he was searching us. Soon, the ordeal was over. The policeman thanked my father and let us go.

My dad let out a sigh. We watched the officer's car pull out ahead of us before my dad started the engine and turned on his signal to re-enter traffic.

"Racist," I mumbled under my breath.

"Hmm," my father murmured as he pulled out into traffic. "That may be true. But not in the way you probably think. You've heard of DuBois? Went to Fisk University and to Harvard, just like John Hope. You remember when your mother and I took you to meet Dr. Franklin? That's how you got your middle name, you know." I suddenly remembered the comic Mr. Douglass had given me.

"Well, for DuBois it's like this: you got two worlds. Two lives. You got your personal world and your professional world. Your home world and your school world. And the hard part is, you're part of *both* worlds. You have to follow the rules to the different worlds at different times—*and* stay true to who you are."

I thought about what my worlds were, and whose rules I had to play by in each. I had the world at home (which I really was not trying to think about right now), the Lia world, the school world, the Douglass world, the Dad world, the Mom world, the Kelsey world. . . They all had different rules. And I didn't know the rules.

I spent the rest of the afternoon at Dad's office, where I was able to borrow a plastic knife from the kitchenette on his floor to finally make my sandwich. Or should I say sandwiches. I made four. From the windows in the conference room, where I liked to hang out, I could see my school and even hear the bells between classes. The wall was almost nothing but window and in the center was a massive wooden table, bounded by high back leather chairs. This was where the NC Mutual executives met and there was a large speakerphone set in the center. When I was younger, my dad let me dial up some friends and connect them together with the conference phone. I doubt he would let me do it know.

I don't think I ever told my dad, but I was proud of him for what he had accomplished professionally. As the Vice President for Operations, he rated a corner office with dark wood paneling everywhere, built-in bookshelves, and his own round conference table for small group meetings. There was even a picture of him, my mom, and some other company leaders with Barack Obama when he was first running for the presidency. It was a natural for Obama to visit there—NC Mutual was one of the first major African American businesses and had been at the heart of Black Wall Street in Durham.

I reached into my bag to pull out my folder for History so I could keep working on my paragraphs about the Wilmington Massacre in the curriculum for Douglass, but when I opened the folder, I saw the comic book again.

I opened it up and began to read about the life of this great historian. The drawings were pretty accurate, too. I recognized some of the scenes from what I'd tried to read of the autobiography on my own, but this was much easier to understand. When I got to the part about John Hope and his mom on the train, I slowed down to examine every drawing.

IT WAS ON ONE OF THOSE TRIPS THAT I HAD MY FIRST EXPERIENCE WITH CRUDE ROLE RACISM. ON OUR WAY TO CHECOTAH, WE FLAGGED DOWN AS USUAL THE SOUTHBOUND KATY TRAIN.

AS IT MOVED AWAY WE SAT DOWN IN THE COACH WHERE WE HAD BOARDED.

WHEN THE CONDUCTOR CAME THROUGH, HE OBSERVED THAT WE WERE SITTING IN A WHITE COACH AND ORDERED US TO THE NEGRO COACH.

MY MOTHER AS FIRMLY SHE COULD REFUSED TO DO SO...

...OBSERVING THAT SHE WOULD NOT TAKE TWO SMALL CHILDREN FROM ONE COACH TO ANOTHER IN A MOVING TRAIN.

SHE POINTED OUT THAT IT WAS NOT HER FAULT THAT THE TRAIN HAD STOPPED WHERE SHE COULD NOT BOARD THE SO-CALLED NEGRO COACH.

THE CONDUCTOR THEN STOPPED THE TRAIN, NOT TO LET US MOVE TO THE SEGREGATED COACH, BUT TO TEACH US A LESSON BY EJECTING US FROM THE TRAIN ALTOGETHER.

WE TRUDGED BACK TO RENTIESVILLE THROUGH THE WOODS.

JUST SIX YEARS OLD, I WAS CONFUSED AND SCARED. THE USELESSNESS OF MY MOTHER'S REASONABLE REFUSAL TO ENDANGER HER CHILDREN, THE ARBITRARY INJUSTICE OF THE CONDUCTOR'S BEHAVIOR, THE CLEAR POINTLESSNESS OF ANY OBJECTION ON OUR PART, AND THE ACQUIESCENCE IF NOT APPROVAL OF THE OTHER PASSENGERS TO OUR REMOVAL, BROUGHT HOME TO ME AT THAT YOUNG AGE THE RACIAL DIVIDE SEPARATING ME FROM WHITE AMERICA.

AS I CRIED MY MOTHER PROMPTLY REMINDED ME THAT WHILE THE LAW REQUIRED US TO BE KEPT SEPARATED FROM WHITES AND USUALLY PLACED IN INFERIOR ACCOMMODATIONS, THERE WAS NOT A WHITE PERSON ON THE TRAIN OR ANYWHERE ELSE ANY BETTER THAN I WAS. SHE ADMONISHED ME NOT TO WASTE MY ENERGY BY FRETTING BUT TO SAVE IT IN ORDER TO PROVE THAT I WAS AS GOOD AS ANY OF THEM.

This was sounding a lot like what my dad just went through being pulled over. Only it was on a train instead of a car. Yet my dad reacted the same way as John Hope's mother. . . "not to waste energy fretting but to save it to prove yourself as good as any of them."

And then, with renewed energy, I set to work on my theories about why our curriculum had failed to include a full account of the struggles of race in our state.

- 7 -

When five o'clock rolled around, I started packing up, but Dad was in the middle of something. I stood at the door and waited for him to wrap up. He suggested I get a ride home with Melinda, who lived down the street from us. He'd probably be there for hours longer. I acquiesced and walked down to Melinda's office. She knew the drill.

"He's working late again?"

"Yes, ma'am," I said, forcing a smile.

I tried to keep conversation in the car to a minimum. The day had been a bit too eventful to speak of, so when she asked me why I had come to the office so early, I just told her it was an early release day, hoping she wouldn't catch on. She didn't.

After I'd let myself into the empty house, I hauled my books upstairs and prepared for a run. Even though there was no need, I opened the creaky windowsill that seemed so much louder now that my parents' voices weren't invading the entire house. I clambered onto the roof, jumped down the pergola, and set off into the light breeze, running at a steady clip.

I just wanted to be free—away from all the commotion of life. I observed the greenery of Trinity Park, and listened to the laughter of small children.

The blur of brightly colored houses passed by. I saw a mother and her two children sitting at the park table tucked inside a vine-covered gazebo. It was getting late and the mother began to pack up their things.

I didn't have a specific direction of where I was going, and that didn't bother me at all. It seemed to be just like my life today: running away, but not knowing who I was running from, where I was going, or even what I was going to do once I got there.

As I continued on my journey, I focused on the beat of my feet pounding against the pavement. I felt sweat run down my temples and drop off of my chin. I pumped my arms, making myself go faster and faster until my breath became hoarse.

I found myself running toward the skate park. The park was perched on a slope overlooking the evolving Durham Central Park. It was carved out of old warehouses and now featured the popular Farmer's Market, a Craft Fair, children's playground, and a long brick wall from Durham's tobacco warehouse days. In the summer, they sometimes showed movies on the wall. And the skate park was deliberately built across the street from a Durham Police substation.

When I got there, I paused to drink from the fountain and watch guys around my age skateboarding. They seemed to be on a pro level. Tre-flips, railstands, you name it and they were landing the tricks with a level of ease that would seem to belong to that of sponsored skaters. I observed in awe at how the boys rode switch and pushed away with so much vigor, and when they decided to heelflip off of ledges, the pop was so loud that the couples walking through the nearby park turned to look, and they went so high in the air that it seemed like they were fifty feet above my head. After someone would land a trick, the people around, knowing the skater or not, would applaud. If they happened to fail, the other skaters would pick them up and continue to help with tips. It was almost like a family.

"Ayy, Parker!" A familiar voice caught my ear.

Shawn looked natural here, his Diamond hoodie in the grass behind him, his oversized white t-shirt billowing slightly in the breeze. But, seriously, anything would look oversized on him. "You're still alive!" he said, extending his hand for a shake. "What went down with Reynolds? What'd he do to you?"

"Ten days," I sighed, taking my time to breathe and look around. Shawn responded with an expletive. "Yeah, it doesn't make any sense."

"If it was me, I'd expel you for bringing crunchy peanut butter into my school. You should know by now, it's creamy all the way, son. Have I taught you nothing?" He paused a moment, as if shifting into his philosophical mode. "It's probably some racist BS. You should fight it." I thought about his suggestion. My dad did have a friend who was a lawyer. Charlie.

"You gonna stay for an afternoon sesh or naw?" asked Shawn.

"Nah, maybe another day," I replied, feeling deflated as I thought of the responsibilities that lay ahead. "I'm gonna head home."

"Alright man, I'll catch ya later," he said, and pushed off onto the bowl.

I began to jog lightly again, still not fully recovered from the vigorous running I had been doing before. My knees ached, but I had to make it all the way home. Soon enough I had run the length of Foster Street, picked up the trail under the railroad bridge, and was back in my neighborhood. When I saw a few girls from school walking down the sidewalk, I waved and put on a big smile. They glanced my way, but no reply came. They just went back to cheerfully chattering to each other, indicating they didn't want to acknowledge I was there.

As I ran up the hill on Markham, the streetlights just now flickering on, I smelled someone grilling—and it was my dad. I couldn't recall the last time Dad had grilled. And I couldn't believe he was doing a normal fatherly thing, especially since our intense exchange earlier that day. The blood orange tint of the sky showed that I had been gone for longer than I'd realized. I felt a pang of guilt. He was trying to make it up to me. All day he'd been trying. To make up for yelling at Mom and yelling at me and working too hard and letting his son run away from him.

I approached the grill and cleared my throat to catch his attention. Suddenly his eyes darted toward me and he put on a stifled smile. He started to walk toward me as if to give me a hug, but then faltered, trying not to ruin the moment. In that instant, we nonverbally said we were sorry to each other even though neither of us was completely ready to forgive.

Then I smiled and said, "So whatcha cookin'?'

"Hamburgers. You want some?" he asked hopefully.

"Yeah, I'm starving," I replied as we sat down on some bright, weatherworn plastic chairs that were too small for us. We sat uncomfortably in those tiny chairs while we ate our guilt burgers and chatted about football and other things that were irrelevant, a relief from the chaos of our present lives.

t was my first day of the suspension, and when I opened my eyes with the sun instead of with the ridiculous jolt of my alarm clock, I was disappointed to be reminded of what I couldn't do. The streaming sun lit the posters of Usain Bolt, who'd rocked the Olympics for Jamaica this summer, and Jesse Owens, who'd shocked Nazi Germany with his wins in 1936 Berlin. If I could be as successful, as humble, as fast . . . But Mr. Douglass had said at the beginning of the year that if you got suspended, even before the season started, you couldn't be on the team—not cross country, not track.

For the next few hours my room became my cage. Dad had gone to work, Mom was gone, and I was here. My only form of entertainment seemed to be sneaking on the desktop and watching past fights on worldstarhiphop.com and taking continuous looks at my texts. My Facebook wall was filled with questions—"Where are you?" "What happened???"

I evened out my thoughts with my iTunes playlist, a library filled with old Outkast songs and some Gorillaz, which matched my current state of mind. Now, visions of laughing with my teammates and awkwardly flirting with the girls on the side of the track seemed to be filled with melancholy instead of happiness. As a matter of fact, these things I had once loved now vexed me.

When my father came home for lunch, he cast a glance into my room only to find me rereading the first chapter of John Hope Franklin's autobiography—the one without pictures. I'd grown discouraged again, and Dad walked in when my mind had drifted off to see his only son buried in a mixture of covers, unwashed clothes, and emptied Hot Pocket wrappers, which had filled the room with a scent not even Febreze could fix.

"You're coming with me," he sighed.

Father and son, we made our way up the steps of the NC Mutual building. As usual, I said hello to Mrs. Johnson, the front desk clerk. I walked to the elevators. Upstairs, I stopped by to say hello to Melinda and Dad's other office mates. I walked into the empty conference room. For the next several hours, I read, did make-up work, wrote and rewrote my paragraphs for Mr. Douglass. I lost myself in the day's activities and the activities—or sometimes non-activities—of the days yet to come.

Taking a break, I stretched and stood next to the window, staring down on some kids at the nearby city bus station. The door creaked behind me. The silent room had made the sound louder, and I startled. It was Dad. "Come here, Kendrick. You have a visitor."

I wondered if it was Mom and whether she was here to yell at me, hug me, scold me, and maybe take me out to lunch. When we reached the end of the hall, which led to my dad's office, I saw someone sitting in one of the two upholstered chairs opposite his enormous desk.

"Hey there, Kendrick."

"You remember Charlie, Ken. He's going to help us fight this suspension."

I sighed and pulled my hood over my head, embarrassed my butter knife had become a civil rights issue, embarrassed my father had to do my bidding. Dad gestured to the other chair, and I flopped down.

Charlie thumped me on the back. "It's okay, son," he chuckled. "Can't always do the right thing." I rolled my eyes and let out a smirk. I thought about Shawn's creamy peanut butter remark.

"So Buck, let's get down to business. We're gonna have to work hard for a delay." He was talking about what happened after the ten-day suspension. When I'd be sent to the alternative school.

Charlie had always been close with my parents. He was even in some of the wedding pictures in the hallway at home. I tried to imagine Charlie twenty years younger. In my imagination, his hair grew out two inches into a conservative Afro, and his face thinned. But there were the same smiling eyes and the same outdated glasses, wire-rimmed with the bar across the top. I'd always liked Charlie. He had a warmth I wished my dad could learn.

I looked around, half listening, half wondering what Mom was doing right now. Hopefully laughing with the other doctors on the floor, checking in on patients, smiling.

"Kendrick," my father said, bringing me back to attention. "Charlie wants to know if you pointed the knife at anyone." I shook my head. It seemed as though Charlie were already familiar with the case. He even had a copy of the referral and a list of extensions written down. "Ms. Curnitt x 33657." I looked again at my father and Charlie as they discussed the next steps. Had they been working on this all morning? While I was in bed feeling sorry for myself?

I watched as my father and Charlie figured out how to delay the suspension. I answered questions once in a while, but most of the time it was just Dad and Charlie. The day felt long and my eyes started to feel heavier every second. As I shifted in the plush chair, my stomach began to rumble.

Taking a small glance at Dad, who was on the phone, and Charlie, who was on his laptop, I slowly stood up and snuck down to the break room. *Walking isn't the same as running, but it is nice to be on my feet,* I thought. Slowly making my way toward the other end of the hall, I overheard many conversations. Endless talking of work, conferences, and "What are you doing tonight?" It was always a bit strange to be the teenager at the office. As I passed open doors, I got everything from excited waves most people save for toddlers to disinterested stares at the tall distraction in track pants.

I spent some time going through the fridge and cabinets, where I managed to find an apple, a granola bar, and a water bottle. Satisfied with my plunder, I walked back to the office to find Dad and Charlie staring at me just as I'd taken a big, loud crunch of the apple. I let it hang in my mouth for comic effect, trying to lighten the mood. I waved with the hand that held the granola bar. When they continued to look confused, I snapped off a mouthful of the apple, and with a shrug I mumbled out, "I was hungry."

Looking back at his work, my father said, "Kendrick, don't talk with your mouth full, son."

Making my way back to the chair, I finished devouring the apple and began lining up my three-point shot at the trashcan across the room.

"No," my dad's voice boomed. Charlie reached over to the trashcan behind him and put it under my nose for a minute. I dropped in the core and began unwrapping the granola bar. I was midway finished when the ringing of a telephone made me stop. My dad picked it up and passed it to Charlie.

"Charlie Johnson speaking." There was a long pause. "Yes, I understand. Thank you very much. Good-bye." Dad and I watched Charlie hang up with a wide grin on his face.

"Congratulations, we delayed the suspension. And you're going back to school tomorrow, young man."

"Really?" I sat up, unconsciously wrapping up the rest of the granola bar. A wave of relief washed over me. And then a wave of guilt. My father and Charlie had spent their day on this, and after constant calling and emailing with the school district's Central Office, they had finally won the administration over. This long day at the office was paying off, but inside there was still something missing—something that I didn't see. That, and I was still hungry.

Dad and I walked out of the big building over to his car. *I still see those kids across the street. I wonder how much fun they've had today*, I thought, trying my best to ignore them as I got into the passenger seat. As he drove, Dad tried to make conversation, but it wasn't working. I answered each of his questions with a one-syllable answer. I was feeling grateful, but still ashamed of my actions. I didn't know why I felt guilty—I hadn't done anything wrong. But after today, I felt like I was marked as a bad kid. I felt like I needed to do something to deserve this punishment. After the drive, I got out of the car and walked up to the front door. Turning the brass knob, I was welcomed by the sound of emptiness and Dad's rattling keys behind me.

That night, he would order us Chinese and we'd eat it while watching college football on the couch. It turned out he was pretty good at parenting when he needed to be.

- 9 -

"Hey Kendrick," Oliver leered as he stepped into my path.

Well, I'm back, I thought as I tried to avoid eye contact. I started walking, and he followed by my side.

"Can you even spell suspension? Probably not since you're dumb enough to bring a knife to school." I sighed aloud and my face screwed up. I dipped my head and continued walking away fast. I quickly looked back and walked faster down the hallway as Oliver continued to stare me down.

That morning, I fielded questions about why I was gone with ambiguous answers. I still felt guilty for something, I still felt like I'd done something wrong. Thankfully, Kelsey hadn't asked any questions. In fact, she'd even said "Hey" to me, which made my heart race.

But it wasn't until lunch that I let my frown turn to a smirk for Lia as I unzipped my lunch box and pulled out a complete, already-made peanut butter and jelly sandwich. "Would you believe it, my dad actually was late to work because he stopped me on my way out the door to ask me if my sandwich was in one piece."

I told her about the confrontation with Oliver that morning and the lingering feeling of guilt. "It's so weird," said Lia, unzipping her own lunch box, which was packed with a variety of vegetables in tiny Tupperware containers. "You two used to be so close."

"Yeah, I mean, you remember in middle school when we were, like, almost real friends. We did everything together." I struggled to unscrew the top of my silver thermos, which I'd filled with coffee that morning. "Oliver spent more and more time with Grant and Kyle. One day apparently they told him he had to choose between them or me. And he did. Why did he pick them?"

Her eyes surveyed me silently as if she was sizing up how much I'd changed in my one day out of school.

Lia didn't seem to have an answer to this, but instead extended her palm. I wordlessly handed her my thermos. She took it and struggled for a few seconds before feeling the sudden click as the lid started turning with her hands. Lia handed it back to me.

"Thanks," I said. She nodded her welcome.

"But Ken, you have to understand where he's coming from, too. He must have felt so conflicted to have to sacrifice his best friend in order to belong with the popular kids." Someone else might be offended their best friend was feeling empathetic toward the "enemy," but I knew Lia and I knew her empathy toward Oliver didn't take away from her empathy for me. Lia was the kind of person who could relate to anybody and everybody. Whether it be a homeless person begging for food or a snobby teenager insulting her "so last year" shoes, she just understood. And that's all I needed at this point.

I took a sip of coffee. I'd decided it would make me feel more mature. Of course, I'd put in enough sugar to make it palatable. Now, it warmed me with its sweet and bitter tang. I turned my eyes to Lia again. "Want some?" Her eyes surveyed me silently as if she was sizing up how much I'd changed in my one day out of school. She was thinking something, but I wasn't sure what. I started to feel a bit weird, so I waved my hand in front of her face, something she did to me when I zoned out. She seemed to shake it off for a moment before returning to advice mode.

"And Ken, you've got to remember your parents aren't perfect. They've got time-consuming jobs and lives to live outside the house—"

"Well, my mother is living her entire life outside the house—"

"Oops, yeah, wrong choice of words. It sucks that your mom moved out. . . But hear me out, I'm not saying it's good they don't always listen to you, but you've got to cut them some slack. They're people, too. Plus, we've both got it pretty good. Some kids at our school don't have *any* money for lunch. Have you ever thought about them?"

I looked away to the rest of the room. I saw Shawn across the cafeteria with some of our skate park friends. He pointed at me and winked. I thought about how Shawn wore the same sweatshirt three days a week and always got lunch from the cafeteria. Elsewhere, kids milled around, talking to different friends, throwing stuff away into the large gray trash cans interspersed between tables, and walking to tables with white Styrofoam lunch trays in their hands. My classmates talked of anything and everything, seeming completely oblivious to the real life matters and situations we discussed.

# # #

After filling in a concerned Mr. Douglass after school, I walked to the public library to do homework until my dad was ready to leave the office. I liked going there to feel more grounded and to get away from the drama at the school library, which everyone called the Media Center. Plus, I thought I might run into Oliver if I stayed at school. I took deep breaths intermittently. I learned this from my mother who always seemed to use this technique when my dad stayed at work too late or forgot to pick me up from track practice.

Lia volunteered at the public library almost every day after school, so she'd ridden her bike over right after seventh period. When I arrived, I spotted Lia already behind the circulation counter. She motioned for me to come over and then told her supervisor she was talking a homework break.

"So how's Kelsey?" she asked, squinting her eyes as she listened.

I thought about how Shawn wore the same sweatshirt three days a week and always got lunch from the cafeteria.

"I'm sorry, Kendrick," Lia continued. "That wasn't very nice of me."

"It's fine. You're right. It's not that big of a deal."

"You really like her, don't you? Aw, that's so sweet." Lia poked her lips out, closed her eyes, and held her face. When she looked up, I had already walked away. "Kendri-i-i-ick," Lia dragged out behind me.

I turned back to see her eyes on me with that far-away look. I wondered what she was thinking about. She sighed and turned away, returning to the counter.

We walked to our spot with the old rickety chairs and the dusty table-top, the same table we had been sitting at since sixth grade in the back corner of the teen section. This was our table and everyone knew it. Lia was the one who picked it, right about the same time her mom passed. She had said it looked sad and lonely, and then she burst into tears. I felt bad and had cleaned it off with a tissue, and we have been sitting there ever since.

In the corner of the library doing my homework I looked sad and lonely, too. Lia and I had been friends since elementary school, but it was times like this where I thought, *What did I get myself into*? I decided my best friend couldn't even handle my thoughts about the girl who turned me down. I was alone. Alone like my mother in her bed shedding tears over the absence of my father. Alone like I always was in my room with the sound system turned to the max in attempt to drown out the sound of my parents' harsh words. I tried to clear my head by pulling out the John Hope Franklin book.

 THERE WAS ANOTHER LONG SILENCE. THEN HE POINTEDLY ASKED...

 DO YOU THINK YOU'LL BE LYNCHED, BOY?

 THERE WAS NO SAFE ANSWER.

  ANY REPLY WOULD'VE BEEN A CHALLENGE. MUTE, STILL, I WAITED.

 ONE OF THEM FINALLY SAID SOMETHING THAT I DID NOT HEAR...

 ...BUT IT MUST'VE BEEN AN ORDER OR A SUGGESTION THAT THEY SHOULD NOT BOTHER WITH THE LIKES OF ME.

 THE LINE BROKE, I WALKED SLOWLY TO THE CAR...

 .. I GOT IN AND RACED BACK TO SWEET POTATO HILL.

 BREATHLESS, WITH NO TASTE FOR ICE CREAM, I TOLD "CHIEF" THAT I COULD NOT POSSIBLY STAY IN MACON ANOTHER NIGHT.

HE QUIETLY TOLD ME THAT HE WAS ALREADY PACKED AND WAS WAITING FOR ME TO RETURN TO TELL ME THAT HE HAD INDEED VISITED THE PLANTATION HE HAD BEEN WARNED AWAY FROM THAT MORNING.

How could something so simple and child-like as ice cream be interrupted by such a threat? Here, I felt like *I* was being singled out, but it was nothing compared to this scene in the ice cream shop. It reminded me of a scene we'd just read in *To Kill a Mockingbird* for English when Atticus Finch and Tom Robinson, in the jail cell behind him, are surrounded by that same U-shape of men with shotguns. But it's his kids that make the men turn away. I hoped to have that kind of calm and courage if anything were to happen to me, or my father, or even Lia. There is wisdom in children like Scout and Jem, I thought. But I wondered if I had it.

A familiar voice interrupted my musings and I quickly shook off the scene with the near lynching of John Hope and my thoughts on Harper Lee.

It was a familiar, sweet, loving voice. *Kelsey*, I thought with a huge smile appearing on my face. *I didn't know she came to the library.* She seemed to be browsing here in the teen section. *Maybe I can recommend something.*

I was about to approach her when I saw Oliver bring her a book. I ducked and hid behind the nearest shelf, hoping I hadn't been seen. I quietly crouched down. I watched for a while, telling myself this wasn't happening. That this was a dream. That when I woke up, this will have disappeared.

Kelsey was laughing harder than she normally did. I thought about the smile on her face when she saw Oliver. The way she twirled her hair whenever he talked. How she hid her face to keep her blushing unnoticed. The way their eyes locked and kept the other in a daze. I had watched it all over the past week in History. How had I not noticed until now? I knew what was happening. I knew what was to come. I just didn't want to accept it.

I packed my things up and headed toward the bathroom, just next to the front entrance, for some more deep breathing.

"I'll be right back, Kelsey, okay?" I heard Oliver's voice behind me. "I just need to check on something."

I heard knuckles cracking as the door swung open. I started washing my hands, to make it seem like I wasn't just in here breathing at myself in the mirror. I looked up and saw Oliver strutting toward me. I had some of the same feelings as John Hope being cornered with his ice cream. But fortunately this was one on one. I exhaled and readied myself for the taunts.

"Hey, Dark Chocolate," he said. "What were you doing back at school today? I thought you were alternative school material."

"Um, my lawyer got the suspension delayed."

"You had to get a *lawyer*? Can't you solve even a single problem without bringing someone else into it?"

"What do you mean?"

"I heard you asking Kelsey for help. Sounds like you think it'll be easier if you've got a girl on your side."

"Me, ask Kelsey for help? I was *offering* her my help, which *she* didn't accept."

"Well, luckily for me, she accepted *mine*. How's that going to *help* you, Kenny G?"

He was in my face now. I tried to look away, tried to hold back my fear I was going to lose control and get in even more trouble than I was already in.

"You mad about something? Maybe you're mad that everyone thinks you're a little bitch. And I know who started it. Your 'best friend' Lia told everybody you're a little crybaby bitch," he said with confidence.

All of the sudden, a rage took over my body. I pinned him against the wall. But Oliver squirmed out from under my hand and slipped coyly out of the bathroom. *Breathe. Breathe. Breathe*, I told myself, thinking about the rhythm and what Mr. Douglass would say.

Reality set in. If I had punched him, my life would be horrible. My friends would desert me and I would disappoint my mom and dad. How did John Hope keep his calm? I slowly backed out of the bathroom and ran out of the library. I would've said bye to Lia, but she was busy.

– 10 –

My breathing eased down a bit as I stepped out of the library. My knuckles started to have a pale color as I clenched my fist tighter from the memories of just moments ago. And then I started running, backpack and all, as if running would do anything. Running from all my problems and not facing them like I swore I would every night.

All I wanted to hear was my feet slamming the ground, but all I did hear was Oliver's voice. I ran until I felt as if the bones in my feet would disintegrate if I took one more step.

Then it hit me. I needed a plan. I needed to know how to make things right with Kelsey, or at least make up from what had happened. As I slowed down to a walk, the sounds of skateboards and teenagers lured me toward the skate park again. In addition to great skaters, the park was also commonly used by students that played hooky and young smokers, ranging from the ages of twelve to twenty. I used these people as an example of what to be and what not to be. Thankfully, I was about to hear from the 'advice guru.'

"Ayy, Parker!" I stopped staring at the tips of my shoes and looked up to see Shawn. He also knew everything about everyone. He could help. As if reading my mind, he said, "I hear you're having lady problems? Right?" He pointed at me and winked before dropping the act and walking over to sit down on a bench.

"Yeah," I admitted, "but—"

"So what type of girl are you tryin' to impress?"

"Well..." I hesitated, still trying to get Oliver's voice out of my head. "I don't know..."

"What is she like?"

"Oh," I sigh. "Pretty, popular, likes sporty boys, she's every boy's dream, she's white—"

"Boy, if you want a white girl, you're gonna need more than dance moves. You're gonna need skate moves. Then once she goes black, she'll never go back, dude." I wasn't sure if I could even begin to articulate how racially problematic that all was, but I did know that I needed help. So I let him put me on the board.

"First, what you're going to want to do is push the board. Since there are a lot of drops, every drop you go into you have to slightly bend your knees." On my first drop, my skateboard dove before I even knew I was at a drop. After the fifth try, my knees were still shaky and I surely looked a fool. *I'd better stick to running*, I thought. I walked to the nearby bench and sat. Shawn was soon beside me.

"Man, I just can't focus on anything with all this Kelsey stuff. Plus my mom's been gone. Do your parents ever fight? That's normal, right?"

"Um, I mean, if they're fighting all the time, it's probably not worth it. But it still sucks. Think about it this way. My dad left my mom, but he comes 'round every so often to see us. It's like me and my mom are a vaca-

50

tion house and he's only a vacationer. No, there's no fighting, but it's almost kind of worse."

"I'm just stuck right now, you feel me?"

I felt like a different person around Shawn, but in the best possible way. He didn't seem to have an ego and he seemed genuinely interested in helping people.

"You love your mom?" Shawn asked.

"Yeah," I said.

"Then that's the support she needs, yo. She needs to know you love her. Now get up on that board and keep tryin' or your mom's gonna be the only girl in your life, and we don't want no Oedipus junk up in here! I'll pick you outside the library tomorrow at five, and we'll get everything straightened out."

The next afternoon, I stomped down the steps of the library towards the grassy lawn. The aroma of sticky pollen wafting through the fall air made me gag. That's when a horn beeped causing me to look up.

A red-rusty 1987 Impala pulled up in front of the library, blocking the traffic behind it. A familiar face from the driver's seat rolled the cloudy, class style windows down. Shawn poked his head out showing his mischievous grin. "Yo, Kendrick come 'ere." Shawn was probably the only ninth grader with a driver's license. But that may be the only benefit of having failed ninth grade once.

I automatically jogged over to the passenger side, opening the old school metal handles and climbed in. The original leathers seats were torn and worn out. The back seat had cans of different energy drinks, bags of empty takis, and a few dirty hoodies. Shawn sat in the driver's seat looking through the smeared rearview mirror. The cracked radio was turned to G105, pumping the tunes of Fabolous's "Throw It in the Bag" as the car roared its engine and we pulled away from the old library. I'd left my bookbag with Lia for the afternoon, so I wouldn't have to lug it around for our "plan"—whatever it was. I owed her one.

Shawn, with his eyes on the road, spoke up. "Dude, one more time, articulate your problem."

I shoved my fist in my pockets and laughed dryly. "Oliver. He's stealing Kelsey from me."

I felt Shawn shift the stick and sigh. "Why do you even like her?"

My thoughts shifted as I considered the question . . . "I don't know, man. There is something, though," I replied, unsure of the answer. Shawn swerved as a car almost hit us. As the car screeched to a halt, Shawn cursed under his breath. The smell of burnt rubber and smoke filled the air, making my head hurt.

After a minute of awkward silence, Shawn grinned. "I have an idea to win this chick over."

I turned. "How?"

Shawn stopped at a red light and looked over. "In Highbridge Mall there is a fine jewelry store filled with diamond necklaces and stuff. We can steal one. Just throw it in the bag," he sang along to the song.

I nodded in understanding, until the realization hit me. "Steal? Stealing leads to jail and jail means I ain't got a life and, all things considered, I am actually okay with my life now. It just doesn't sound right."

Shawn shook his head. "Don't worry, it's easier to steal than to pay. Plus, we'll be all Robin Hood, stealing from the big corporations to give to the people. I'll help you," stated Shawn, convincing me to go along.

Shawn swerved into the parking lot. This sudden motion made my head collide into the side window. I sat there holding my head and a weird taste of metallic liquid filled my mouth. My lip stung. "I bit my lip," I said, almost to myself.

We walked to the entrance from the parking deck. The huge food court smelled of pizza and other warm, soft things. I suddenly got very nervous when we walked past a large group of people eating at Subway. They all seemed to look up for a minute, stare at me, and then go back to eating their sandwiches. I was afraid they had already figured out that I, Kendrick Hope Parker, was about to steal jewelry from a very expensive and well-known store for a girl that had already rejected me. But I could always trust Shawn.

This was so unreal. I wasn't from a family that steals. Why was I even considering this? I couldn't imagine what would happen if I got caught. *My dad might even leave me in jail to teach me a lesson*, I worried.

But if I succeeded, I was sure to win over Kelsey. If I didn't succeed, she probably would stay far away from me. My palms were sweating and my heart felt like it was racing. Did I really want to make choices like Shawn that might land me in jail rather than walking across a stage with a diploma in my hand?

Shawn pulled me along as he zigzagged through a crowd of people. *Why is it so crowded on a Thursday afternoon?* I thought to myself. As soon as we were near Macy's, I stopped suddenly and stood still, like a statue in a park.

"What the heck is wrong with you, boy?" asked Shawn "We have been through the plan at least seven times and you still seem scared."

"I dunno. I just feel like I'm going to get in trouble," I replied

"Well, if you do, I got your back." While Shawn said this, I started to think.

"Maybe, we could just save up for the money to buy a sweet gift. Then we wouldn't be doing something wrong and it would be perfectly legal."

Shawn stared at me as if I was a donkey riding a unicycle.

"Uh, no. Do you know how freakin' long it would take for us to gather six hundred dollars?!" asked Shawn. "Just grab the jewelry and make a dash for it." Even though Shawn's reply wasn't really reassuring, I decided to keep along with the plan. "So, let's review one more time: you pick out the necklace, then you give me a signal—"

"Clap my hands," I said, interrupting Shawn.

"Yeah, then I am going to distract the, um, salesperson." I nodded my head in approval, signaling I knew what came next.

We entered the store and went right to the necklaces. There were so many beautiful pieces that I had no idea what to get Kelsey. They had emeralds, rubies, and sterling silver. As I was scouring for the perfect piece, Shawn called me over. He had found a sapphire necklace. It was a pretty royal blue with three huge pendants. *This will look good*, I thought to myself. "I think we've found the perfect one," I whispered to Shawn as he nodded in agreement.

I called the attendant over. *Show time.*

"OMG, can I try on the necklace right there?" I said, pointing to the sapphire. The woman was skeptical, but willing to humor us, so she reached into the case and presented it to me. I leaned my neck forward so she could clasp it behind my head. I looked in the mirror. Clapping my hands together, I squealed—typical fangirl move.

Shawn's voice interrupted the conversation. "Excuse me, ma'am." The woman's attention slipped right to Shawn. She occasionally looked back at me, but I just batted my eyes into the mirror, pretending to decide whether I wanted the sapphire or not. "Ma'am, do you know how many lives this diamond has claimed?" Shawn said, pointing at a ring. "Yes, that one, right in back. No, on the left. Yes, how many lives has *that* diamond claimed? You know, my uncle died on a trip to South Africa trying to film a fight there."

Lie, I thought, unclasping the necklace and anticipating the moment I could slide it into my pocket. But when I looked around, the mall police looked me right in the eyes. Then, I panicked.

I took off, dropping the sapphire on the glass counter and hearing it slither off onto the tiled floor. The guards were after me. I ran past the Sunglasses Hut, almost knocking the lady over and then cut through the greeting card store. I sped out of the nearest doors, dodged traffic across Club Boulevard, and continued running up Watts Street. With chase scenes from movies spinning through my head, I wove through the service alleys, cringing when some dogs started barking, and cut through yards. I was almost home.

- 12 -

turned off Watts onto Markham, my street, and slowed down to a speed walk, not quite ready to let go of the rush I felt running from the police. I had ditched Shawn, but I knew he had an escape route. Instead of continuing on to my house, I crossed the street to arrive in front of the house I considered my second home. Lia's house was brick like mine, but that was where the similarities stopped. While mine was wide and sprawling, hers was small and cute. White two-by-fours crisscrossed the triangular second story, making it feel like a wonderful grandmother's house. I saw a figure sitting on the steps. Not seeing me approach, she was looking around and absorbing her surroundings, her curly mass of hair blowing every which way in the wind. In that moment she looked majestic and regal. For a minute I had forgotten all of my problems and was focusing on that sweet familiar face. But then, as I hurried up the walk, I remembered why I was moving so quickly.

I set my foot on the stoop and she looked up, smiling vaguely as if not entirely awake. "Scrabble?" she asked. I nodded and she stood up to open the door. This was our ritual: we'd meet on either of our front stoops in times of trouble and let it all out with a furious game of Scrabble where all the words related to what we were thinking about—the only kind of Scrabble two troubled nerds could have.

We walked into the living room. Lia sank down on an old red sofa while I went over to get the box from the bookshelf. I set up the board, avoiding her suspicious glances. As we got our letters she raised her eyebrows as if asking, 'Are you going to tell me or do I have to ask?' I positioned my letters into my tile rack. She sighed and said, "What is it?"

"Everything," I answered without looking at her. I knew the slight smirk on her face wasn't insensitivity; it was the joy of being able to attempt to make a difference for the better in someone else's life. I'd seen this same facial expression every time I had a problem and we talked about it while we played a favorite board game.

"I just almost got caught for shoplifting and ran here from the police, my parents are getting a divorce, and I don't know if the one girl I really like likes me back." Her eyebrows came down to form a glare, and she opened her mouth before I finished.

"I'm sorry, I must not have caught that. Did you say you were *on the run from the police*?" She threw her arms out wide at the end of this sentence as if illustrating just how large my apology would have to be for not telling her this sooner.

"Well, I'm not really on the run. I didn't *actually* steal anything," I said, hoping it would diminish her glare.

"Kendrick Parker! You were considering stealing something? What? Why? Where?" Lia was so mad she had resorted to listing the three Ws.

I told her the tale, starting with Shawn in the parking lot and ending with walking up to her front porch. As I told it, I realized how pitiful I sounded, stealing jewelry for a girl who may not even like me.

"Kendrick, somewhere there is a long list of stupid things boys do for girls they like and I'm afraid you just made the top ten." If anything, her glare got worse. "No girl will ever like a guy who commits a crime in order for her to like him. And if they do, then they don't deserve anyone. And how did you let Shawn talk you into this?"

"I –" I started.

A booming voice from down the hallway said, "Lia! What did I tell you about doing your homework as soon as you got home? And you know Jessica hates cleaning up after you—what's all this mess in the kitchen?" Lia's dad was home from work early. I couldn't see him, but I could hear his voice echoing in the spotless kitchen.

"Dad, I finished all my homework at the library and 'that mess' is me unpacking my lunch box and getting dinner in the oven." Lia and her dad had never seen eye-to-eye, but their disagreements had gotten worse ever since her dad first brought Jessica home. I worried that she and her father would never understand each other until it was too late to say, 'I'm sorry for being so stupid.'

"I can vouch for that, Mr. Farrington. I was there at the library." I knew it unwise to mention how little time I'd spent there. At the mention of the library, Lia pulled my bag over from beside the couch, reminding me to take it. 'Thank you,' I mouthed to her.

"Oh, hello, Kendrick. I didn't realize you were here. Well, you guys, I gotta run. See you at dinner, Lia." I heard the back door slam. He was always either running to or from work. Maybe he thought if he could forget himself in his work. He could forget everything else, too. Second wife and daughter waiting at home. First wife nowhere to be found except in the margins of those books Lia held so dear.

Lia hunched over the Scrabble board, muttering about never being appreciated. I put down my first word, 'smash.' She looked up at the clack of wood against cardboard.

"You know Kendrick, I don't really want to play Scrabble right now."

I guess the magical tell-all-your-fears Scrabble game was losing its touch. I scraped up the tiles from the board and dropped them into the bag, realizing how very sad and empty the sound of Scrabble tiles mixing together was. I put the worn box back on the shelf and stared at the books next to it. There was the usual Lorraine Hansberry plays, a couple Richard Wrights, and then I noticed a smiling face peering at me from a shiny dust jacket. This was getting too creepy. John Hope Franklin was everywhere! I pulled down *Mirror to America* and flipped through it.

"Hey, it's the hero of my comic book," I said to myself.

Lia looked at me, confused. "The Green Lantern? I don't really see the resemblance."

"No, no. But Dr. Franklin is a hero in a way," I explained. "You know who Jackie Robinson was?"

"John Hope was the Jackie Robinson of higher education," I said. "And both hit pay dirt in Brooklyn. It was front page news in *The New York Times* for each of them when it happened."

"First African American baseball player in the major leagues drafted to the Dodgers in 1947," Lia rattled off.

"So, yes. Well, John Hope was the Jackie Robinson of higher education," I said. "And both hit pay dirt in Brooklyn. It was front page news in *The New York Times* for each of them when it happened."

"I don't get it," said Lia. "What exactly did Dr. Franklin do?"

"He was the first African American to get a teaching position in a white university. He received his doctorate in history from Harvard but the color line was as strong in universities as it was in baseball. Dr. Franklin is also one of the nicest people alive. I can't believe you haven't heard of him before." I swiftly rummaged through my bookbag to pull out the slim graphic autobiography. I flipped through the pages until I found one of my favorite sections and held it out, so both Lia and I could see. "I think you'll get a kick out of his story about making dinner for his wife, Aurelia."

ONLY ONCE DURING THE AUTUMN DID I BREAK MY INTENSE WORK SCHEDULE AND ENGAGE IN AN ACTIVITY THAT WAS FOR PURE PLEASURE: I MADE AURELIA DINNER. SHE WAS OFF PAYING HER PARENTS HER FIRST VISIT SINCE OUR RETURN FROM CAMBRIDGE, AND I DECIDED TO GREET HER WITH A HOME-COOKED DINNER BY CANDLELIGHT.

BUT WE HAD ONLY ONE HOT PLATE AND A SMALL ELECTRIC OVEN THAT PERMITTED ME TO PREPARE ONLY ONE ITEM AT A TIME, I WAS DETERMINED TO SERVE THE MEAL IN OUR APARTMENT.

THE MENU WAS RELATIVELY SIMPLE:

A SMALL BEEF ROAST, WHICH I NEVER PREPARED BEFORE;

SPINACH SOUFFLÉ, WHICH I NEVER PREPARED BEFORE;

MACARONI AND CHEESE, WHICH I NEVER PREPARED BEFORE;

AND DESSERT WOULD BE A FRESH FRUIT COMPOTE, WHICH I ALSO NEVER PREPARED BEFORE.

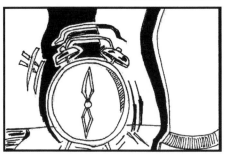

THE WISEST THING I DID ON THAT MONDAY MORNING WAS TO RISE EARLY.

BY THE TIME I WAS TO MEET AURELIA AT THE RAILROAD STATION, THE MEAL WAS TAKING SHAPE.

UPON OUR RETURN TO THE APARTMENT, I HAD ONLY TO ARRANGE THE FLOWERS ON THE SMALL TABLE AND LIGHT THE CANDLES.

A FIVE-STAR RESTAURANT MAÎTRE D' COULD NOT HAVE BEEN AS PROUD AS I WAS OF THAT PRODUCTION, PARTICULARLY GIVEN AURELIA'S COMPLIMENTS TO THE CHEF.

"What a sweet man. Now, Ken, that's how you impress a girl," said Lia. I laughed, still ashamed of myself. "The food probably wasn't great but the gesture was wonderful. I have a feeling they made a great pair."

- 13 -

Before I had left for school that morning, Dad said he wanted me home in time for dinner, so I left Lia's house, grateful for a father who was willing to cook dinner for me.

When I got home I went straight up to my room, still rattled from the afternoon's adventure and feeling that I had to make some changes, and fast. I ran in and out of my room, back and forth to all parts of the house. Now, before me on my bed, lay my new uniform.

Collared shirt and dress pants from the back of my closet. A suit jacket that's too small for my dad that I found in the back of his closet. A skinny black tie from his tie rack. The last piece I had some trouble finding, but I remembered my dad kept his old pair of glasses from college in the cupboard above the fridge.

He went through a black separatist stage back then, closer to the actual time period than I was now. I liked to look at his high school and college photos when I needed a good laugh.

Now I realized I was starting to look and dress like him. The glasses were Malcolm X-style Ray Bans with thin black frames. I didn't need the magnification, so I popped out the lenses and left them above the fridge.

I got dressed in my new assemblage and came down to dinner in it. My dad's only reaction to my new style was a slight raise of the eyebrows and the comment, "Make sure those lenses don't get scratched, wherever you put them."

# # #

The next day, I wore my new uniform to school. I walked into Mr. Douglass' classroom and dropped my backpack down next to an empty desk off to the side of the room. I started to throw myself into the chair as I usually did, but then remembered what I was wearing. I carefully pressed my tie against my chest as I sat down, making sure to keep it from getting caught on the top of the desk. I gingerly lowered myself onto the seat, feeling the shirt begin to loosen from the tight constraint of my waistband.

I leaned over the side of the desk to get my history binder out of my backpack. I flipped to a clean page and positioned my pencil in my hand as the rest of the class shuffled through the door and into desks. When I hunched over my paper to write my name in the corner, the glasses I had put on that morning slipped halfway down my nose. *This*, I thought, pushing them back up with a firm finger on the bridge, *could take some getting used to*. I began to feel sorry for all the people in the world who needed to wear glasses for their own benefit. They slipped back down again.

I decided to keep them there. After all, most scholarly people keep their glasses about halfway down their noses, don't they?

The deafening bell rang. Mr. Douglass took his place at the front of the room and outlined the day's lesson.

"Please take out the paragraphs you wrote a few nights ago. You should have written on why so few people know about the Wilmington Massacre of 1898. Today we are going to discuss these. Now, would anyone like to share their writing?"

A few hands shot up while many kids tried to look invisible. Some did a pretty good job of it, like that girl, Cassandra. She somehow found a way to sit so still and dress in a way that seemed to repel attention. She almost blended in with the furniture, the walls, and the lockers when she walked down the halls. How was that even possible?

"Kendrick? Kendrick..." Mr. Douglass was calling on me. I shook my head to bring myself out of my Casandra Invisibility Mystery, almost sent my glasses flying, and stood up to read my paragraph as my classmates gaped at my wardrobe.

"If you took present day Durham, and transported it back a little over one hundred years, that would be the feel of Wilmington in 1898. The City Council was fully integrated, there was a large black middle class, there was a daily newspaper owned by African Americans, and the town was incredibly prosperous. Most of this success was the result of blacks, poor whites, and liberal whites working together as the Fusion Party to get their candidates elected to office. However, they had some powerful enemies, in Wilmington, and around the state. These people conspired to drive out the Fusion Party leaders. And they did it with armed vigilantes, burning down the black press, and driving the leadership at gunpoint from the town. Wilmington hasn't been the same since. It went from the richest and largest city in North Carolina to the seventh largest with a mediocre economy."

"Thank you, Kendrick," said Mr. Douglass. "And why do you think the Wilmington 1898 coup is not covered in the curriculum?"

"What's the saying about the victors write history?," I said. "It's an embarrassing and appalling legacy. Why *would* the state leaders want this taught?"

"Next up, Shawn. You have a forty-three percent in this class. If you get up and read this paragraph you had all week to write," he stopped and gave Shawn a 'hint, hint,' look, "I will be willing to boost your average to a sixty-five." Shawn stood up. *Here we go again*, I thought to myself. There was a brief moment of silence. No Kelsey giggling, no Oliver being cool, just silence, shortly interrupted by the scooting back of Shawn's chair.

"My paragraph reads," he cleared his throat and put down the paper he had dramatically been holding in front of his face, "I don't do homework. It's a waste of time. I don't do homework, I live on the line. YOLO." The class cracked up. Including me.

"Thank you for that poetic rendition, Mr. Graupner. Now class, you can begin packing up. Remember, if you want extra credit, you can read the book *Crow* by Barbra Wright and write a summary of it. The book should appeal to you. It's the story of Wilmington 1898 from the point of view of a young teen whose father is an editor for Manly's paper."

As I stepped out of the door, the speakers beeped three times, announcing a very apologetic sorry-to-interrupt-class-but-you-really-need-to-know-this announcement. "Teachers and students, please excuse this interruption. A table will be set up in the cafeteria for debate team sign-ups during both lunches."

I had "A" lunch, right after fourth period, so after eating with Lia, I stopped by the table with the giant Debate Team sign propped up next to it. I stepped up to the table and said, "Hello, I'm here to sign up for the debate team." I gave the lady at the table my name and grade.

She checked a list in front of her and said, "I'm sorry, but we only take participants with a clean record. I believe you have some disciplinary actions on your record."

I continued to stand before her, trying to will her with my silence, my composure, my flipping suit and tie. I was trying to channel Dr. Franklin and—*Breathe, Breathe*—not say anything to admit a wrongdoing. But somehow, all I got in response was, "Suspensions are not tolerated."

A tall student, probably a senior said, "Yeah kid, stop holding up the line, boy."

# # #

That afternoon, all my pent-up anger pounded into my legs and I ran as fast as I could to the library. It was hard running when you had a tie flapping in your face every two seconds, but it didn't matter. That lady was so stuck up. I was so embarrassed by the public humiliation followed by the other student calling me "boy." When I arrived, I found Lia and I pulled her over for a second.

"I can't be in the debate team, just because I was suspended!"

"Well, I guess it makes sense for more serious disciplinary actions, but they have to give everyone the same consequences," said Lia.

"I know that, but it just doesn't feel fair."

I slumped at our table, dejectedly paging through the John Hope Franklin book in search of help. Partway through it, I realized there were a lot worse things than being called "boy." I turned back to the beginning of the section with Dr. Franklin going to Montgomery to do research at the Alabama State Department of Archives and History.

MONTGOMERY.
STATE DEPARTMENT
OF ARCHIVES AND HISTORY.

I WAS LOOKING FOR SOME PAPERS ON GOV. WINSTON. THE ATTENDANT INFORMED ME THAT SINCE THOSE PAPERS HAD NOT BEEN COMPLETELY PROCESSED ONLY THE ARCHIVIST, MRS. MARIE BANKHEAD OWEN, COULD GRANT PERMISSION TO SEE THEM. AT THE FIRST OPPORTUNITY I WENT TO MRS. OWEN'S OFFICE AND ASKED THE SECRETARY IF I COULD SEE HER.

WITH THE SECRETARY'S AUTHORIZATION I WENT IN, AND AS I DID I LEARNED TWO IMPORTANT LESSONS OF SOUTHERN ETIQUETTE.

THE FIRST WAS THAT THE DOOR SHOULD NOT BE CLOSED WHEN A BLACK MAN IS USHERED INTO THE PRESENCE OF A WHITE WOMAN.

THE SECOND WAS THAT I SHOULD NOT EXPECT TO SIT DOWN IN THE PRESENCE OF A WHITE WOMAN, UNLESS SHE TOLD ME TO DO SO.

WHEN MRS. OWEN LOOKED UP, SHE ASKED ME QUITE GRACIOUSLY WHAT SHE COULD DO FOR ME.

I ASKED PERMISSION TO SEE THE PAPERS OF GOV. WINSTON.

SHE SAID THAT SHE WAS PLEASED TO GRANT IT, WAS THERE ANYTHING ELSE I WISHED? I REPLIED IN THE NEGATIVE, THANKED HER, AND WAS ABOUT TO LEAVE WHEN SHE SAID...

I HEAR THAT THERE'S A HARVARD NIGGER HERE. HAVE YOU SEEN HIM?

THAT'S HIM.

BEFORE I COULD RECOVER MYSELF SUFFICIENTLY, A VOICE REACHED US FROM THE OUTER ROOM. IT WAS THE SECRETARY, WHO COULD HEAR EVERYTHING, SINCE THE DOOR WAS OPEN.

YOU DON'T LOOK LIKE A HARVARD NIGGER TO ME. HAVE A SEAT.

AS I TOOK THE SEAT CLOSE TO HER DESK, SHE REMARKED THAT NEITHER DID I ACT LIKE A "HARVARD NIGGER". THEN SHE ASKED ME WHERE I WAS BORN AND RAISED.

WHEN I TOLD HER I WAS FROM OKLAHOMA, SHE SHOOK HER HEAD. SHE DECLARED THAT I COULD NOT HAVE RECEIVED MY "NICE MANNERLY TRAINING" IN THAT WILD COUNTRY. THEN SHE INQUIRED ABOUT MY COLLEGE EDUCATION.

WHEN I TOLD HER THAT I WAS A GRADUATE OF FISK UNIVERSITY IN NASHVILLE, SHE EXCLAIMED THAT NOW SHE KNEW WHERE I GOT MY GOOD MANNERS...

...IN A GOOD OLD CONFEDERATE STATE!

I couldn't believe the things John Hope had to put up with. Good thing he didn't bring a butter knife with him to the Archives or he might have been lynched. But what got me even more, as I read further on, was that John Hope and Mrs. Owen later became friends. I guess charm and courtesy are worth something.

- 14 -

Mr. Douglass' question about why Wilmington 1898 was not taught in North Carolina was really getting to me. And getting me angry. From what I read about John Hope Franklin, he didn't stand by when history was being distorted. I needed to write to someone in power but didn't know the right person. Then I thought about the State Board of Education and decided to write to the State Superintendent. As soon as the idea hit me, I sat down and wrote a draft letter. And for good measure, I would copy our principal.

To: robin.douglass@dpsnc.net
From: youngscholar1995@gmail.com
Subject: Letter about Wilmington 1898

Hi Mr. D.,
    Attached is the letter I'm sending to June Atkinson. Can you look over it for me and tell me if I should change anything?
Thanks,
Kendrick

Dear Dr. Atkinson:

My name is Kendrick Parker and I am a ninth grader at Pauli Murray High School in Durham. My World History teacher, Mr. Robin Douglass, recently introduced our class to the 1898 Wilmington Massacre. Often called a race riot, it was the only successful coup d'état in the United States. The Democratic Party in Wilmington forced democratically elected City Council members (both whites and African-Americans) out of office at gunpoint. They then marched across town to the single black newspaper in the South, *The Daily Record*, and burned its offices down. A group of the men took off on a trolley and stopped at a street corner in a black section of town. Across the street from them stood a group of black men. They began yelling back and forth at each other. A policeman ran up to them to calm them down, but it did no good. The white men still held their guns and began shooting at the blacks. By the end of the day, more than twenty black people were dead or injured. Not a single white person was harmed.

This important date is not in any North Carolina public school social studies curriculum so I am proposing that it should be added to eighth grade social studies. We already focus on North Carolina and US history that year, so it would make sense to put it there.

Thank you for your time. I look forward to hearing your thoughts.

Sincerely,
Kendrick Hope Parker

PART TWO

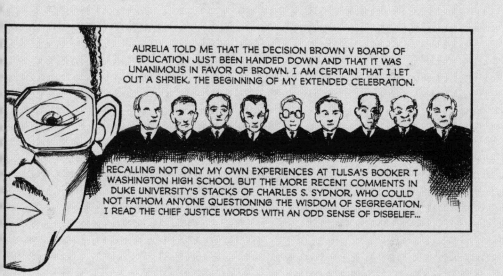

AURELIA TOLD ME THAT THE DECISION BROWN V BOARD OF EDUCATION JUST BEEN HANDED DOWN AND THAT IT WAS UNANIMOUS IN FAVOR OF BROWN. I AM CERTAIN THAT I LET OUT A SHRIEK, THE BEGINNING OF MY EXTENDED CELEBRATION.

RECALLING NOT ONLY MY OWN EXPERIENCES AT TULSA'S BOOKER T WASHINGTON HIGH SCHOOL BUT THE MORE RECENT COMMENTS IN DUKE UNIVERSITY'S STACKS OF CHARLES S. SYDNOR, WHO COULD NOT FATHOM ANYONE QUESTIONING THE WISDOM OF SEGREGATION, I READ THE CHIEF JUSTICE WORDS WITH AN ODD SENSE OF DISBELIEF...

– 15 –

The school year passed as best it could, and before we knew it the cold air began to turn warmer and the spring was nearly upon us. I continued to admire Kelsey from afar through my dad's lensless glasses. She even said hi to me on a regular basis. Shawn and I still hung out, even though I wasn't about to take any more advice from him on girls. What was I thinking, anyway? And by now, I had worked my way through about a third for Dr. Franklin's *Mirror to America* (yes, the one without pictures). Since we're tight and it was only a butter knife, Douglass had made an exception for me with the whole suspension issue and running on the team, so after we closed out the cross country season strong, it was only a few months before track would ramp up.

Let's skip ahead to spring, where things started to get interesting again. The warmer weather woke everyone's inner competition, as if it had been hibernating all winter, and the end of third quarter had us all in a frenzy for summer even though it was still three months away. But it turns out, we hadn't grown up this year as much as we'd thought.

It was after school, the day of a big track meet, and everyone was feeling jittery, especially me. I was nervous throughout the whole day. In math, we had a unit test and I couldn't concentrate no matter how hard I tried.

Everyone at our school had been waiting for this since the season started. Coach Douglass had been telling everyone around the world about it. He even posted pictures of the flyers he made on Twitter to his (surprisingly) hundreds of followers, so just about everybody in Durham turned up. I had already talked to Lia to see if she was coming. She gave me a yes. Shawn said he would drive over with Vic from his math class. Knowing Oliver was running today, too, Kelsey would probably be in the bleachers, front row. That would be a win-win for me when I would finally show that garlic-breath, pizza-slinging, always-borrowing, pug-faced squeep (I don't think that's a word, but if it was, he would be the definition of it) Oliver that I was faster than him. After a rocky start, I had consistently placed just seconds behind Oliver in every single cross country meet of the season.

After being released early from classes, we headed to the locker room, to pick up our gym bags, uniforms and cleats in tow. In there, I saw Johnny and his crew talking about the 4x4 relay they were running later.

"Ay, yo, Kendrick, I heard you picked up those new Eric Koston shoes," Johnny said.

"Yeah, Diamond Blue Colorway," I replied.

"Oooh, that's gonna kill everybody at school. With that suit, too. That is legit!"

"Hey, check this out," Tony exclaimed as he walked up to the group. He then showed us a contact on his phone with the name Chantelle Gilbert on it.

"No way, the captain of the cheerleaders gave you her phone number?" Johnny said.

"Yeah, plus that's not even a 919 number!" I added. We all laughed.

And then Oliver came. He stopped in front of me and made a point of looking me over from top to bottom.

Oliver said, "Whoa, excuse me, but did I just travel back to the 1920s?" He'd been making fun of the outfit for months. I was surprised no one else had gotten sick of his routine. This time, though, my nerves were fried and I'd had enough.

"I see you really know your history Oliver," I said, "or are you too white to even recognize the style?"

Before Oliver could respond, Mr. Douglass was there, urging everyone on the team bus.

As I waited in line to board the bus, I realized I wasn't breathing. *Breathe.* I let it all out, my frustration with Oliver, and my confusion. We were friends before any of this started. We were cool, brothers even. Where had all of it gone? I'd let her come between us. Kelsey had become just another competition to us. All the same, if we were in a race for her, I decided I was coming in first.

I stepped on the bus and decided I couldn't dwell on it now. I had to get my mind right for the meet. As I was walking to the bus I heard him. Oliver was speaking to our long jumper. "She's not even that cute, but I'll get her before he does. I got her in the bag, and I don't even like her that much. As you know, the King gets what he wants."

I stopped and turned back to look at him with disgust. He knew I'd heard him. He probably said it so I could hear him. I thought as my face twitched, *This is a setup. Keep walking.* If I'd learned anything from my father, from John Hope Franklin, it was to keep your cool and walk away. Dad walked away from troubles, pain, hurt . . . and even seemed to run from my mother and me sometimes. As I questioned myself, Oliver's cackle broke into my thoughts. It was getting louder and louder. We boarded and I sat down alone in the front seat, just behind the driver, waiting for Coach Douglass.

Oliver feigned getting out of his seat. "Wait, let me escort you to the back of the bus, nigga. That's where you're supposed to be."

I turned around, and stood up so I could look at Oliver eye to eye. The bus turned from rowdy to extremely quiet. His cheap body spray burned my nose.

"'Nigga'?" I stepped into the aisle and took a step forward. I could feel the eyes of my teammates on me. Oliver spread his arms, showing his chest and gesturing for me to come at him. "Last time I checked, Oliver, we *both* had to brush the naps out of our hair in the morning. You just drown yours in gel, in your failed attempt to be a white boy."

Before I knew it, Oliver was coming at me, those eyes showing the rage I knew he had in him, a rage I felt when I was almost expelled for having a butter knife, the rage of a black man accused of being something he's not.

Now, he was on top of me. Wedged into the tiny aisle between the blue faux leather seats, Oliver gripped my shoulders and rattled my skull against the rubber ridges of the floor. I'd always thought the aisle of a bus was unnecessarily padded, until now. Running shoes moved toward me, empty Cheetos bags and gum wrappers crunching beneath them. A warm, sticky substance trickled down my temple into my ear.

I looked towards Oliver, he cradled his hand to his chest. Tears began to well up in my eyes.

I got up and started backing away, stunned, trying to wipe the blood off my face with my shirt. He tried to take advantage of the opportunity by throwing another punch. But this time I saw it, and dodged. I punched him in the stomach, then another, and a last hit to the gut. He fell to the floor.

My teammates on the bus cheered. I heard a symphony of "Get 'ems," and "Work, K." It seemed as though I wasn't the only one getting tired of Oliver. I sat in a seat closest to where I stood and gingerly wiped off my face with the towel from my bag. I winced, finding the already raised bump above my ear. I'd have some explaining to do when Dad saw the blood stains.

A whiff of cologne reminding me of pine trees announced Douglass' arrival. He had just stepped onto the bus. The noise ceased as if nothing had occurred. "Get up off of the floor, son," Mr. Douglass' voiced echoed. Oliver struggled to his feet, and took his place next to the long jumper.

Suddenly ashamed, I turned to Oliver and whispered, "Are you alright?"

He looked at me with eyes of hurt. "Fine."

Even though I felt bad for letting my anger take control of me, some part of me felt strong. And I wasn't sure how I felt about that. I absent-mindedly grabbed a book from my backpack to distract myself from the scuffle. I'd been carrying around the comic Mr. Douglass had loaned me for almost the whole year now. Its pages felt soft and worn, no longer slick and sharp. I absent-mindedly flipped through it until the word "bus" caught my eye, and I returned to a familiar scene.

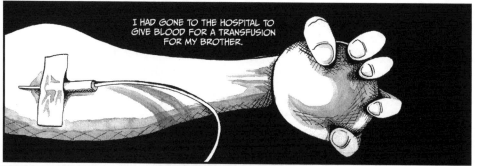

I HAD GONE TO THE HOSPITAL TO GIVE BLOOD FOR A TRANSFUSION FOR MY BROTHER.

RETURNING ON THE BUS, I SAT DOWN IN THE FIRST VACANT SEAT I SAW. THE DRIVER, A WHITE MAN, TOLD ME THAT I WOULD HAVE TO MOVE BACK TO THE NEGRO SECTION.

WHITE

I TOLD HIM THAT I HAD NEITHER THE STRENGTH NOR THE INCLINATION TO MOVE. I HAD BEEN TO THE VETERANS HOSPITAL TO GIVE BLOOD TO MY BROTHER WHO HAD SERVED IN THE UNITED STATES ARMY SO THAT SOMEONE, CERTAINLY NOT HE, COULD ENJOY EQUALITY. NOW, THE BUS DRIVER WANTED ME TO ACCEPT UNEQUAL TREATMENT, AND I WAS NOT GOING TO STAND IT. FROM THE REAR OF THE BUS, THE BLACK RIDERS BEGAN TO CALL OUT, "STAND YOUR GROUND!"

AND WHEN IT WAS CLEAR THAT I WAS GOING TO DO PRECISELY THAT, THE DRIVER SAID NOTHING MORE TO ME. IF HE HAD STOOD HIS GROUND, I FRANKLY DO NOT KNOW WHAT I WOULD'VE DONE, BUT I HAD HAD ENOUGH.

Yes, I had had enough, too. Especially of that slime-ball Oliver. I was going to stand my ground against Oliver and show him quiet strength will win out in the end. I'd been waiting patiently to get back at him.

And then we were at the racecourse at one of the largest public high schools in the city. Before the race, the team huddled up. I tried to be as far away as possible because some people were already sweating from the high knees stretch and warm-up lap around the track.

Up first were the 100-, 200-, and 400-meter races. I was jumping up and down throughout all of them, yelling for my teammates, and trying to figure out a strategy to beat Oliver. Oliver looked calm as ever. I didn't understand how he could be, when he knew I was going beat him—and not with my fist this time. When it was time for the 800, we took our places, me in lane two, Oliver in one. The gun went off and Oliver went for it, sprinting as fast as he possibly could, which was dumb on his part. He was far ahead of me for almost two whole laps, which made me nervous. I remembered what my dad said to me right before the race: "Save all your energy for the last part, and wow the crowd."

As soon as I remembered this, I looked into the crowd and saw Kelsey, which didn't help me become any less nervous. There wasn't much time left and slowly I gained on Oliver. He must have heard my feet slapping on the track because he looked behind him with a nervous expression on his face.

I wanted it so bad. I wanted to show Kelsey and the crowd I could beat Oliver. And so I went for it. I didn't notice the crowd, or hear anything; I just felt the wind on my face, stinging my cut as I zoomed to the finish line. Cheers brought me back to reality. The loudest voice I heard was Kelsey's. "Yeah! Go Kendrick!" Seeing the big smile across her face, I couldn't help but smile myself.

I walked off the track, my grin widening with every step. My eyes were fixed on Kelsey's. She ran up to me. "That was great, Kendrick!"

"Thanks!" I replied. I wasn't sure what else to say, distracted by the sweet scent that followed her everywhere. Whatever she was wearing, it worked.

After the meet, I walked onto the already-filled bus, but got no recognition there. Everyone who had just cheered for me was now crowding around Oliver, filling him with remarks like, "What happened out there, Oliver?" and "That little skimp shouldn't have beaten you!"

I pointedly sat in the front row, smirking at Oliver. Unfortunately, Oliver caught the look. He glared at me, which I must admit was a little creepy. A glare is more dangerous than a punch. If you get punched, the person just lets out all their anger on you. If they glare, you know they're planning something, but don't know what. I looked away, feeling his eyes boring into the back of my head.

When the bus arrived back at Pauli Murray, Mr. Douglass caught me as I was heading into the building. I could tell he had something to say.

"I was very impressed with your strategy in that race, Kendrick."

I replied, "Thanks, I badly wanted to win." We walked together to the front parking lot where our parents were waiting to pick us up.

"Listen, Kendrick. I really like the letters you have written to the legislature and DPI. I would like to work with you to write more about what you think. That would show those people in Raleigh there are young students out there who care about what they are taught."

I agreed to work a little bit more on the letters. But I wondered what else could be done to really get their attention.

- 16 -

"Hey, Lia." I leaned over the counter as she checked out a few books for a girl who looked around seven. The girl was missing a front tooth and her hair was up in two pigtails.

"There you go, sweetie," Lia crooned, handing the little girl back her books. "So . . . You beat Oliver yesterday. Good job!" She smiled. I puffed out my chest, not even realizing what I was doing.

"Why, yes I did, thank you."

She pulled out a sheet of paper. "Let's see. So if you ran the 800 in 120.88 seconds and Oliver ran it in 123.98 seconds, then you had a 3.1 second difference. Then if you divide each of those times by two—" I leaned back against the counter, letting Lia ramble and scanned the kids' section. I heard a familiar voice and looked over to the reading corner on the rug. There sat Kelsey, reading *Olivia the Pig* to a group of little kids and looking as beautiful as ever.

She looked up and saw me. I looked away, embarrassed, my hand straying to the bandage above my ear. When I glanced her way again, she was smiling at me. I smiled back and she waved. I let out a very, very masculine sigh and looked at my fingernails and put on a bored face. I was sooo playing this off. I looked back up.

My head echoed with *She invited me to her house, she invited me to her house, she invited . . .* until I told myself to just shut up.

"Ken?" Kelsey was suddenly standing in front of me.

"Oh. Hey, Kelsey. You like reading to the kids?" My voice came out a little squeaky and I cleared my throat. I saw Lia turn around to push a cart of books to the stacks, flashing me a thumbs up.

"Yeah, I love kids. I come here every week to read to them. I'm surprised Lia hadn't told you." I looked back at Lia, now walking away. "Hey, I was just wondering if you wanted to come over tonight for dinner. I've already asked my parents."

I shrugged, playing cool. "Yeah, sure."

"Okay, I'll see you then!" she said, bouncing on her heels.

There was no way I could concentrate on my homework after that. My head echoed with *She invited me to her house, she invited me to her house, she invited . . .* until I told myself to just shut up. I figured the only way to get this out of my head was to jump into someone else's. And John Hope was handy.

DURING MY FIRST YEAR AS A BOY SCOUT, AGE 12, I WAS IN DOWNTOWN TULSA AND SPIED AN ELDERLY WHITE WOMAN HESITATINGLY ATTEMPTING TO CROSS THE STREET.

IT WAS OBVIOUS THAT HER SIGHT WAS IMPAIRED AND I RUSHED TO HELP HER, THUS FULFILLING THE BOY SCOUT REQUIREMENT TO DO ONE GOOD DEED EACH DAY.

SHE EAGERLY ACCEPTED MY ASSISTANCE.

HOWEVER WHEN WE WERE IN THE MIDDLE OF THE INTERSECTION AND EXCHANGING PLEASANTRIES SHE ASKED ME IF I WAS WHITE OR NEGRO.

NEGRO.

WHEN I REPLIED THAT I WAS NEGRO, SHE SHOOK HER ARM LOOSE, COMMANDING ME TO TAKE MY FILTHY HANDS OFF OF HER.

REALIZING THAT FOR HER MY RACE DEFINED MY CLEANLINESS AS WELL AS MY ABILITY TO GUIDE HER SAFELY ACROSS A BUSY INTERSECTION, I LEFT HER STRANDED IN THE MIDDLE OF TRAFFIC.

I CANNOT SAY THAT I'M DEEPLY HURT BY THE EXPERIENCE, FOR MY MOTHER'S ADMONITION WHEN WE WERE PUT OFF THE TRAIN SOME YEARS EARLIER REMAINED WITH ME. ALTHOUGH SURPRISED, I DID NOT FRET. I WOULD PROVE, IN DUE COURSE, THAT HER COLOR OR RACE DID NOT MAKE HER ANY BETTER THAN ME OR MY PEOPLE.

"Wow," I said to myself. I silently cheered John Hope's response to the racist old lady. But for a moment I wondered how he would have felt if the old lady got hit by a car while crossing the rest of the street.

$$- 17 -$$

Kelsey lived in a big house, one of the biggest in our neighborhood, which is saying a lot because it's a pretty nice place. I tapped the golden knocker against the door as I fiddled with the pink bowtie I had taken so long to pick out. *Is this too casual? Should I have picked out something more appropriate?* I thought.

I had picked out this one because I knew that pink was Kelsey's favorite color. *Am I being sweetly attentive or stalkerish?* As these thoughts bounced around in my mind this dinner started to seem like the worst idea since the Shelbys sold Tom in *Uncle Tom's Cabin*. I started to rotate the heels of my Cole Haans when the door swung open.

"Hey," Kelsey said, seeming out of breath, her face bright red. *Wow, she even looks gorgeous when frazzled*, I thought. "Sorry it took me so long, I was tidying up a little."

"No, it's fine. I completely understand."

"Well, come on in," she gave me a wide smile while she held the mahogany door with inlaid glass patterns. As I stepped inside, I craned my neck in awe at how incredibly high the ceilings were.

When I looked back down, a short, fat man in a suit was standing in front of me. He cleared his throat. "And who might this be?"

"Dad, I told you I was gonna have a guest over," she responded with that angel voice of hers. Her dad pulled her into a nearby room. I could hear him angrily whispering about how he was expecting a nice, handsome, and intelligent boy like Oliver and not someone like me. Kelsey came back and sat down on the couch, motioning me to sit beside her, just like nothing had happened in the ten seconds before that.

To make things more interesting and less awkward, I attempted some small talk. "So what are we having for dinner?" I asked.

"Oh, I don't actually know . . . Are you hungry?" she asked nervously. Before I could answer she speed-walked to the kitchen. I sat down uncomfortably on the L-shaped leather couch next to the kitchen doorway. I could hear what sounded like Kelsey's grandmother fussing about how I needed to be patient. Kelsey came back with a ceramic platter of cheese and crackers.

"Sorry it took me so long," she said as she pushed the platter into my hands.

"But . . ." I started to say, but realized Kelsey was looking very flustered.

"Sometimes my family just drives me nuts!" said Kelsey. "Ugh, it's show time," she whispered as her apparently blind grandmother was steered into the living room by Kelsey's dad and settled into a chair.

"Greeting young man," said the courtly voice.

"Greetings to you, young lady," I responded in kind.

"How nice of you to say that," said the grandmother. "I don't know if my charming granddaughter told you, but my main interest these days is politics. Did she warn you?"

"No, Kelsey must have forgotten," I said. I worried where this was headed, but I didn't want to be rude about it, so I entertained the conversation. Surely, this would be something about the Purple Hat Society or maybe Medicare if I was lucky.

"Please forgive an old woman's bluntness if I ask you something," continued the grandmother. "Did you vote in the last election?"

"No, ma'am," I said, "I wasn't old enough. I will definitely vote in the next presidential election, though."

"I was mighty disappointed, myself," said Kelsey's grandmother. "I think John McCain really deserved to win. He has so much more experience than that negro boy."

Kelsey winced and looked apologetically at me. I decided to let my gaping mouth hang open for just a moment more before raising my right hand to my chin to close it. Kelsey's father then whispered something into his mother's ear, surely about me.

I sat in shame as Kelsey's grandmother proclaimed her disappointment in Kelsey for bringing home a "negro." The way she said this was as if I was some type of wild animal she didn't want around her or her granddaughter. While Kelsey and her grandmother argued with each other, I began to disengage from the conversation and fortify myself by recalling Du Bois' idea of double consciousness.

I went over Du Bois' quote in my head, which I had memorized after my dad had shared the idea with me: *It is a peculiar sensation, this double-consciousness, this sense of always looking at one's self through the eyes of others, of measuring one's soul by the tape of a world that looks on in amused contempt and pity. One ever feels his two-ness—an American, a Negro; two souls, two thoughts, two unreconciled strivings; two warring ideals in one dark body, whose dogged strength alone keeps it from being torn asunder.*

I thought of what Kelsey's grandmother said referring to me racially instead of who I was. While all of these thoughts scrambled in my head, I remembered the day my dad got pulled over and searched by the police.

I was transfixed in my thoughts, until a strange vibration in my pocket brought me back. I looked to make sure neither Kelsey nor her grandmother was paying attention. I gently slid my phone out of my pocket and saw it was Lia.

I didn't want to make a bad impression, so I ignored it, and looked up. Kelsey cut her eyes at me very strangely and said, "Hey Kendrick, are you okay?"

I replied by nervously clearing my throat. "Yes, yes, I'm fine." Kelsey's parents looked at each other oddly and then looked at me. I started to look around, acting like I didn't see them staring at me. As I took a visual tour of the living room, I began to notice their belongings in more detail. There was a marble light blue table with a strip of gold surrounding it. The chairs had nice fancy designs on the back of them. I had never seen anything like it. I started feeling out of place.

"Excuse me," I said to Kelsey. "Can you point me to a bathroom?"

As I hid there catching my emotional breath, I tried to remember bits of another Du Bois passage I had read. I said it softly to myself, at least the parts I could remember, as I looked into the mirror in this home where I was not welcome: "I do not wish to Africanize America," I whispered. "I won't bleach my Negro blood in a flood of white Americanism. I simply wish to make it possible for a man to be both a Negro and an American without being cursed and spit upon by my fellows—or my fellows' grandparents—" I added, "without having the doors of opportunity closed roughly in my face."

I was shocked at how cold and unwelcoming the world could be even from someone as innocent-looking as Kelsey's grandmother.

While I was in the bathroom responding to Lia, I got a text from my mom saying she was back at the house picking up some things to take to her sister's, where she had been staying. I hadn't seen her in a week, since she'd been out of town on a trip for the hospital.

Kelsey came back and sat down on the couch, motioning me to sit beside her, just like nothing had happened.

I walked back into the dining room. "Hey Kelsey? Can I talk to you a minute . . ." I paused. ". . . outside?"

She nodded and blushed furiously. As soon as we closed the door behind us, she started crying. "I'm so sorry, Kendrick! I should have warned you, they can be so insensitive, but really they don't mean anything by it. Oh my God, you must think we're horrible people, and I don't blame you for wanting to leave, 'cause that's what you brought me outside to tell me, isn't it?" She sighed and sat down on the front steps, burying her face in her arms. I sat down, too, and put my arm around her cautiously.

"I was going to tell you I need to leave . . ." She groaned softly. ". . . but," I said quickly, "it's not because of them. . . It's just . . . Well . . ."

She lifted her head up and looked at me in her cute, confused way.

"My mom just texted me. She's at home and . . ."

She gasped. "Oh, Kendrick, I'm sorry. Of course you have to go!"

The storm clouds started to drizzle, and I stood up to leave. It suddenly started to rain lightly. "Wait!" she said, and then blushed shyly. "If you're going to leave, at least let me give you this," she whispered. Then she leaned forward on her tiptoes and kissed me, ever so gently on the lips. My heart started pounding. I could almost smell her vanilla lotion through the wet rain. She pulled away and said ever so sweetly, "Bye, Kenny."

I somehow managed a wave and stumbled through the rain toward my house.

came into the house breathing heavily, my eyes darting ahead, looking for Mom. I found her in the living room, collapsed into the brown love-seat with her feet propped up on the coffee table. Her eyes were closed, emphasizing the bags under them. Mom always used to complain about me stomping down the stairs, and what had started as a way of teasing her turned into habit. I felt bad for waking her. I quietly tried to sneak out of the room.

"Ah, Kendrick, come here and have a seat. I've missed you," said my mom as she patted the cushion beside her. I walked over and leaned my head on her lap and gazed into her eyes. I had missed my mother. A lot. She adjusted her bun and she said, "You've been dressing quite differently this year. It's not the usual t-shirt, sweatpants, and basketball shoes every day. But you look pretty sharp, my man! You okay?"

"Yeah, Mom. Don't worry about me, I'm fine. I guess I just want to look good. Maybe it'll make the girls like me more," I said.

She stroked my hair and said, "Oh, I see it's that kind of matter, huh? Who's this special girl?" she asked as she straightened my collar.

"Kelsey . . . I don't know if she actually likes me though. I'm pretty sure she's all for Oliver, the biggest jerk in my grade. Besides, a pretty girl like Kelsey would never really like me."

My mother looked at me skeptically. "Huh. Don't worry about Oliver or Kelsey. Girls will like you for you. Did she not just invite you to her house for dinner?" asked my mom.

"Kendrick, trust your own mother. I promise that invite was a start!" She reached out her hand for my cheek. I shied away, yet relished her comforting touch. "You know, she didn't have to do that, but she chose to."

"Yeah, you're right," I muttered.

"It may not seem like it, especially now, but there was a time your father and I were in love. In fact, he looked just like you. Short haircut, slender, straight teeth, and bright eyes behind those huge glasses. Almost every day after class, we'd sit on the same worn green couch in the student center and read poetry. We had dozens of fantastic times together reading poetry. But over time and changed circumstances, we just drifted apart. People change, and that's okay. Don't get me wrong, Kendrick, I still do—and will always—care about your father. After all, he did give me one of the greatest gifts I've ever received." She squeezed my arm. "You. So for now, just listen to my words: keep your friends close, have a blast with them every time you see them, and never, absolutely never, take any one of them for granted. Got it?"

"Uh, I guess so . . . It just feels like so much is going on right now."

"It'll all pan out, my friend. And always remember to relax, be you, and live life without worrying. But I'd better get going. I love you, Kendrick," she said as she gave me a hug, leaving me lingering with the scent of the coconut shampoo she often used.

"I love you too, Mom. Thanks."

I walked upstairs and idly lay on my bed, staring at the ceiling, thinking about what my mother had said. Those were the words I had needed to hear. The front door slammed from down below. She was gone.

was still in bed when I heard Dad's car bottom out at the end of the driveway and then pull to a slow stop. I'd felt energized by the conversation with my mom, so I bounced my way downstairs to welcome Dad. He was looking tired, but seemed heartened to see my enthusiasm.

"You won't believe what happened at Kelsey's house," I said.

"I would love to hear," said Dad. "Just give me a second to unload this stuff. And maybe bring out a bowl of the pistachios."

I went into our giant pantry and found the pistachios in the back corner. I poured some into a bowl and brought another bowl for the shells. I was thinking how similar Dad and I were, like how they both had to be doing something with our hands while talking. Pistachios were perfect for this. Peeling oranges worked, too.

We sat at the dining room table, where my father slid in catty corner to me. "So what was cooking at Kelsey's house?"

"I really couldn't tell you what was cooking for dinner," I said, "because I left before dinner was served."

"Oh, my. This is going to be an interesting story, isn't it?" Dad cracked a pistachio and its shells clinked into the bowl.

I told my dad about the comments from Kelsey's grandmother and how I didn't take the bait, just kept playing Du Bois in my head. About how I'd left early to see Mom.

"So how did Kelsey respond to that?" asked my father.

"She understood, I guess. She also apologized for her family's behavior, and then . . ." I held my father's gaze for a moment in a dramatic pause. ". . . gave me a kiss as I left!"

My dad laughed. "Your head must be spinning."

"And I had a really nice talk with mom before she left," I said, trying to change the subject after having ventured into the awkward region of talking about girls with my dad.

"I'm really glad to hear that," said my father. "I can tell you've been missing her. Hey, I'm also proud of you for how you used Du Bois for help keep you calm.

"I have another story for you which might be a good image for the future," my dad continued. "It's actually from John Hope Franklin. A friend of mine, Art Padilla, had a pond where John Hope loved to go fish. One day Art came home and saw John Hope there by himself. He had come there straightaway from the Raleigh-Durham airport, still wearing his suit pants and tie, but with his white shirtsleeves rolled up. Of course he knew he could come out any time he wanted, but it was unusual for him to be dressed that way. When Art asked him, John Hope said he had just come back from one of those meetings of the Commission on Race Relations that Clinton had appointed him to. John Hope gruffly explained he just had to come fishing after a horrible meeting where they had 'beat up' on him . . . But then the line jerked, and suddenly all was well.

"Art said he had many fond memories of their conversations as he watched John Hope 'harvest' the pond. He would always explain, as he reeled in fish after fish, that the pond needed 'harvesting' so the bigger fish could really grow . . ."

I let this sink in for a moment as I struggled with another pistachio. What needed harvesting in my life? What needed to grow?

Dad interrupted my thoughts with a laugh: "But Art said he always thought that was a crock, and told John Hope so, too."

-20-

had a plan. Sprouted after the evening talking with my parents, the plan would help me put in perspective what was important to me. Plus, Douglass and I hadn't heard anything back from the Department of Public Instruction for months now. Good thing I knew someone with a car.

"I just gotta clear my head," I'd suggested to Shawn. "And what's more calming than looking out on the endlessness of the ocean? Plus, after all this research on Wilmington, I'd kind of like to see where it all happened. And we have that teacher workday tomorrow. What else are we gonna do?" Shawn was obviously game, though I nixed his idea of getting a hotel and cutting class for the rest of the week. Lia was easy; I had her at the word "beach"—and also the words "historical" and "tour."

And now here they were, picking me up at eight o'clock on a Wednesday morning when we didn't even have to be awake. I said goodbye to my father, who was being remarkably cool about this whole thing, just as he was about to leave for work. I bounded down the steps of my house, heavy gym bag in tow, just as Lia was doing the same across the street. We playfully argued about shotgun for a minute until Shawn snapped us out of it. "Lia, you're up front, girl," Shawn decided, reaching over to push open the passenger side door.

Once in the back, I remembered why it was so hard to ride with Shawn. My nostrils were overwhelmed by the old car's rotten-egg smell. I coughed into my fist.

I slowly cranked down the window and soon fresh air filled up the vehicle. "When you gonna clean your car, man?"

"Hey, lay off. Your trashy attitude will damage it even more, dude."

Lia laughed as she adjusted her own window. She looked back at me for a moment, blushing, and turned to look at the landscape. The color of the car faded into an orangish yellow as the morning sun glanced off the hood. Shawn didn't know the route, so Lia and I navigated. After we were on I-40 East, going past Raleigh, we didn't have to give Shawn directions anymore. We just watched the city landscape gradually transform into cotton and tobacco fields before sprouting back up into strip malls as we neared our destination.

I tried to explain to Lia and Shawn about my project with Mr. Douglass, and how our trip would be part relaxation and part research. All through this, I kept thinking to myself, *Should I tell them? Do they need to know why we're really going to Wilmington?* I couldn't answer it confidently so I decided to keep my mouth shut.

# # #

We finally arrived in Wilmington around 10:30. Lia would not quit bothering me about going to the beach.

"Can we *please* go to the beach?" Lia said, more of a demand than a question.

"No, we've been in the car for two and a half hours and I'm really, really hungry. Plus, it's too early right now. Maybe we can go later in the afternoon," I told her. And anyway, going to the beach right then would mess up my plans for the day . . . not that I was going to tell them about that.

"Okay, okay . . . I guess I can wait. There's a coffee shop across the street—I bet they have food." She didn't even wait for us to answer before she opened the door and got out of the car.

We followed suit and began to walk down the street. Shawn excused himself to go skateboarding—he'd been looking forward to exploring some new spots. "Wait!" I called after him, his wheels already lighting up the street with sound. "I forgot something in the trunk!" I let Lia go ahead without me and I ran to get my bag with Shawn. I lifted it carefully, trying not to let anything rattle.

"Just some books for the research I'm planning on doing while we are here," I explained to Shawn preemptively, loud enough for Lia to hear. When I caught up with her, she said, "That's a pretty big load of books for a day trip, Mr. Speed Reader."

"Well, you have to be prepared. Plus, it feels light to me. I've been working out. Wanna feel these muscles?" I put out my arm for Lia to feel.

"Goodness, Kendrick," Lia said, poking my arm.

I told Lia I'd meet her at the coffee shop in a moment.

"I'm going to get the tickets for the historical tour before they sell out. See you in a few." I looked in the coffee shop before I walked away, just to make sure Lia would be okay by herself. The shop had a modern touch to an old style—very homey.

I walked across the street to where they sold tickets for the tour. It might have taken a little longer than I expected because there was a church bus full of children that got in line just before I did. There had to be at least fifty of them. I hoped they wouldn't distract us while we were on the tour, because I knew how kids could be.

I saw Lia from across the street through the window graced with letters spelling out Hypno Coffee. She distractedly ran her fingertips along the crown of her head as her other hand caressed the edges of the pages. She had brought Charles Chesnutt's *The Marrow of Tradition*, which we'd both read now, and had been doing dramatic readings of our favorite sections aloud in the car. Yes, this was definitely my best friend.

As I crossed the street to the corner, I saw myself reflected in the shop windows, my tie flapping against my face in the wind. I pushed open the door to the coffee shop and was welcomed by the smell of freshly baked cookies and soft muffins. Lia was curled up in a window booth with a mug of steaming tea clasped between her two hands. She was so absorbed in her book that when I slid down next to her and said "Hey," she jumped, spilling tea on her book and me. We both erupted into giggles.

"Kendrick Hope Parker, don't you *ever* do that again!"

I laughed and pulled out the three tickets to the race riots tour as I asked if she'd seen Shawn. It was 11:20 and the tour started in a mere ten minutes.

"He's still off vandalizing some innocent building with his skateboard," she huffed, pushing over her a half-eaten bagel and an Arnold Palmer that she'd ordered for me. I devoured the bagel with a haste I soon regretted.

Mouth still full, I mused, "Well, it's not vandalism if it's a message for the public good, right?"

Her eyes flashed on me questioningly, before she shook herself into a smile. "You mean, 'Down with the man'?"

We both silently agreed to keep reading as we waited for Shawn. I opened up to one of the key moments in the illustrated John Hope autobiography to steel myself for what was ahead.

I yearned for my own victory in Wilmington and in the State. I wanted my own shriek of disbelief as the State Board of Education finally acknowledges that Wilmington 1898 should be taught. It took forever from the original Supreme Court ruling on "separate but equal" to the reversal with Brown v. Board of Education. It was over a hundred years since the 1898 Massacre, so surely we were due for our own reversal by the higher powers in Raleigh.

As I fantasized about my own sweet success, Shawn burst in with ruddy cheeks and messy hair, holding his skateboard.

"Bro," he shouted, attracting some annoyed looks from those around us. "The skate spots around here are boss. We gotta go to the skate park later."

"Sure, man. Okay, guys, ready to be educated?" Shawn shifted his board from one arm to the other. "Lia, try not to make the tour guides feel stupid."

Lia looked at me, almost offended. "Sure, I'll do my best impression of a sweet colored lady."

It took forever from the original Supreme Court ruling on "separate but equal" to the reversal with Brown v. Board of Education. It was over a hundred years since the 1898 Massacre, so surely we were due for our own reversal by the higher powers in Raleigh.

"Okay, okay, there's no need for an attitude." I laughed as Lia rolled her eyes, packing up her books. I heaved my bag onto my shoulder, again trying my best to do it carefully so it wouldn't make any noise. I'd spent all my savings on the suit, so I didn't have enough to buy a new pack to match. I felt just a little silly with my gym bag full of what I was telling my friends were history books. We walked out of the shop.

These moments of freedom must have looked awkward to everyone else: a gangly child in a suit with a rattling sports bag and frames without lenses, a Doc Martin-wearing girl reading *The Marrow of Tradition* and drinking Earl Gray tea instead of doing AP Biology, and a gawky-looking skater, with short hair that still managed to look messy, who disturbed the peace of that Wednesday morning with the rattle of wheels on the cement.

I handed our tickets to the tour guide and looked around. The rest of the group consisted of a bunch of old guys with too small shirts and some Asian college students. I guess the church group was doing a later tour.

"Hello, everyone," the tour guide said a little too cheerfully. "My name is Bill Walters, and I'm going to be your tour guide today." Yup, definitely too happy. I felt bad at the thought of ruining this guy's day.

He took us to the front of the building where the mob gathered and forced the City Council members out of office at gunpoint. We next walked the route to where Manly's newspaper building once stood.

"The mob arrived here and proceeded to burn down the building. Luckily, someone warned Alexander Manly, and he was able to get away from the building in time. Men were also posted along the outskirts of town, making sure Manly didn't leave alive, though they weren't sure exactly what he looked like. Manly headed out of town in a carriage and almost made it before his horses were stopped by vigilantes. These men, however, mistook him for a white gentleman, gave him a gun, and told him to shoot Manly if he saw him." The tour group chuckled slightly at this.

We arrived at the site of *The Daily Record*, but were only aware of this fact because the tour guide told us as we stood staring at the blue-gray gravel parking lot next to a church. "You'll notice there is no marker here, no plaque. I'm not even sure the members of this church realize the significance of their parking lot."

We traveled on, deeper into the neighborhood, until Bill called a halt at the intersection of two streets. "The mob dispersed after a while, and a lot of the men went home. They took the trolley into the neighborhood and got off at this corner. The men had been drinking and held guns in their hands. Across the street stood a grocery store. Some African-American men stood in front of it and the two groups of men started calling back and forth across the street at each other. It escalated into yelling and soon a policeman ran up, trying to calm them down. He disappeared soon after, not having made a difference. The white men then began shooting at the black men. They tried to run away but were shot in the back and died in the street. One man crawled under the porch of the house diagonal to us and was only found after he died, when the smell began to set in.

"Many of the African-American women living in the city took their children and hid out in the swamps for the night. In the end, twenty African-Americans were injured or killed, but not a single white person was harmed."

Our fearless guide started the group up the street, heading to the Wilmington 1898 Memorial. I had looked up the site online before we came. Gigantic paddles were set in the concrete, symbolizing the voyage into the next life. I figured I'd have to see it later.

I caught Lia's arm as she passed and leaned in to whisper, "I'm going to call my dad and check in, 'kay?"

She nodded absentmindedly and watched the group head down the street. When they were far enough away to no longer see clearly, I did what I had to do, and then pulled out my phone and dialed two TV stations.

"We're standing here live with Kendrick Hope Parker, a high school student from Durham, and the young man behind this radical act of vandalism. Or is it activism? At this intersection in downtown Wilmington, outlines of bodies have been spray painted onto the streets and sidewalks around us, along with a message reading, 'The historian is the conscience of the nation.' Mr. Parker, what is your reason for doing this?"

"Well, ma'am, I want to make people aware of those murdered in the Wilmington 1898 Massacre; no one learns about this in school, either. So, I'm asking the State of North Carolina to update its curriculum to mirror the reality of our American history." As I continued to explain myself, two more reporters pulled up to the scene.

Then came the question, "What inspired you?"

I thought back the people who had wormed their way into my everyday conversations. "John Hope Franklin and W. E. B. Du Bois really made an impression on me. Those two people have a big impact on the way I think now. And the quote about the historian being the conscience of the nation? That's Dr. Franklin himself."

The world buzzed on around me, cameras clicking and flashing like the fireflies and crickets I used to catch. I spotted Lia and Shawn and the rest of the tour in the crowd. Soon, my friends were cleaving through the group of onlookers to get toward me. People backed away from me as I walked toward Lia and Shawn. They stared in amazement at the spray painted figures.

"Why didn't you tell us?" Lia asked, and then dismissed my answer before I said it. "Do you think you'll get in trouble? You're on the news! How long ago did you plan it?"

Shawn clapped me on the shoulder with respect in his eye. A sharp buzz shattered our portrayal of three best friends at an enlightening moment. I slid my phone out of my pocket and unlocked it. It actually was my dad this time.

"I just saw you on the news." I held my breath. "I'm proud of you, Kendrick," he said. My heart soared up and up toward the sky—and was promptly shot down by the sound of sirens.

A police car pulled to a stop on the street just a few feet from us. Two officers opened the door and walked toward me.

"Kendrick Parker?" asked the taller of the two. He had a scruffy beard and glasses.

"Yes," I answered. There was no point in denying it. No point in running now. This was something I had come to stand for.

The other officer spoke. He was clean-shaven, with a burn mark on his arm. "You're under arrest for vandalism and disturbing the peace. You almost caused several accidents back there." He pushed me into the back of the car, but I felt like he was being a lot gentler than he would be with most criminals. In the commotion, my phone dropped to the ground. Lia picked it up and handed it to me. Our hands briefly brushed and then the door was slammed shut. *Funny*, I remembered thinking, *how ironic it is, disturbing the peace on a former riot site.*

- 22 -

Everything comes with a sacrifice, I thought, *especially if I am in the back of a police car with handcuffs on.* There was a cage separating the policemen and me. The car was silent except for the radio calls. I don't think I'd ever felt as alone as I did in that backseat.

Maybe I went too far. Maybe I shouldn't have done what I did. Well, it's too late now, I thought as we arrived at the station.

The booking clerk asked my name. "Kendrick Hope Parker," I replied.

"Age?" she asked.

"Fifteen," I said.

"No way," said the arresting officer. "He's at least seventeen."

The clerk was clearly bored by this procedure and asked for some ID. I reached into my pocket and realized I had given my wallet to Shawn to hold. "I asked my friend to . . ."

"Looks like we'll have to book him as an adult until his father can get here from Durham," said the clerk with a grin.

Since I didn't have five hundred dollars to post the bond, the police officer took me to a holding cell, the sight of which made my heart pump faster. "You can sit on the bench right there and wait for your father," the assistant said. He closed the barred door in front of me and locked it with a heavy set of keys. The two left and I slowly went to the dirty bench to sit.

I looked around. The holding cell's bars were silver with ugly colored spots. The bench was metal and freezing cold. Fading paint chipped and peeled off the walls. The cool air tasted of metal, dirty clothes, and cigars. On one side of the cell, I saw a hole, like someone had punched the wall.

I couldn't see the jail from where I was, but every once and a while, someone was brought back in from the visitation room and the door would swing open and I would hear the chatter of the prisoners. One man was singing "The Word Freedom." Another argued with an officer. "I didn't do it, man!" "Of course you didn't," came the response. Another black man they brought in was wearing ripped and dirty clothes. I could smell him twenty feet away. I kept looking around until my eyes stopped on a random object. They were collecting his personal belongings in a side room across from my cell. He had a picture in his hands of what looked like his family.

That word, family, kept repeating in my head. Family. My separated family. My divorced family. I didn't want to hear or see anything, so I covered my eyes and ears. I wanted my father to get here quickly so I could get over with the police questioning me and get out of this place.

There was a small TV in the room near the holding cells. All the police officers watched, and passed their time listening to the news. It felt like hours just listening to the silken-voiced reporters talking on and on. Nothing seemed to catch my attention.

A familiar voice sounded from the TV: "We're standing here live with Kendrick Hope Parker, a high school student from Durham, and the young man behind this radical act of vandalism. Or is it activism?" A different voice began. A man. "Kendrick Parker spray-painted outlines of bodies onto two downtown Wilmington streets, claiming his interest in raising awareness of victims of the 1898 Massacre. Parker is a freshman at Pauli Murray High School in downtown Durham. The school was named for the Durham-raised civil rights activist Pauli Murray, whose pacifist participation in sit-ins for racial justice seems to have influenced other Durham youth. Like Murray, who was the first African-American woman to receive a Yale law degree, Parker is a star student who, earlier today, attempted to take his studies—to the streets. Let's take another look at what happened at the scene."

I wasn't upset about what I did. I was more proud than concerned. Yes, I was a tad worried my dad might kill me. Also, to think what my school would say, having one of their students sent to jail. I don't think this would win over Mr. Reynolds.

I paid attention to the reporter, taking pride in what I was about to say in response to my actions. "Everyone deserves to know what happened here in Wilmington in 1898. It upsets me that so few people do. This is something that everyone needs to learn, particularly young people, but it is not taught in our schools. All I'm doing is trying to get things moving along."

The male announcer continued. "This young man, Kendrick Parker, says he spray painted outlines of several who died during the Wilmington Massacre in 1898. He was taken by the police a short while after the incident. Sources tell us he is currently being held at the New Hanover County Jail."

I stopped listening after that. I was hoping all this would be worth it, that it would catch someone's attention and help move along the NCDPI petition. Every man and woman who died during that terrible tragedy deserved to have their story told. Why keep them silent?

The formal voices returned to my ears. "We interrupt this program to bring you the following breaking news. It was just reported that the distinguished historian Dr. John Hope Franklin has died. He suffered from a congestive heart failure at the Duke University Medical Center. He was ninety-four. Dr. Franklin will be missed for his outstanding work in Afro-American studies. More on this story at six."

All the thoughts running through my head suddenly vanished. There was nothing left for me to ponder. I just sat there, in the holding cell . . . waiting for my reaction to catch up with what I just heard.

John Hope seemed like he would live forever. Even at ninety-four he was still active and sharp. I needed him more than ever, particularly now, and he was gone.

- 23 -

I leaned against the wall and felt the peeling paint loosen into my hair and fall down my collar. I shook my shoulders in annoyance but could do little else to rid myself of discomfort. Paint chips were at the bottom of my list of important things today. I spread my legs out across the floor, seeing how far they would reach before I began sliding off the bench. Not very far, it turned out. I sat up straight to stop myself from crashing onto the floor. I shifted and turned, trying to achieve the impossible of finding a comfortable way to sit on a bench, in a peeling cell, forgotten in a jail, 156 miles away from home.

# # #

With a jolt, I realized I was sitting in Mr. Douglass' classroom. Well, it looked like his classroom at first glance, but the posters on the walls were different. I realized they were all of people I knew. "Lia Farrington, First African-American Woman President," read one, with a photograph of what looked like Lia in twenty or thirty years. I moved on to the next one. "Robin Douglass, First Teacher to Ever—"

The door creaked behind me. I spun around.

An elderly African-American man was closing the door behind him. When he turned around, I saw that he was wearing a suit and tie, with large wire framed glasses halfway down the bridge of his nose.

"Hello, Mr. Parker," the man said. His voice held years of knowledge, but despite our age difference, I knew he would talk to me as a peer. I was not surprised he knew my name.

"Hi, sir," I answered. And then, because I could not help myself, "I'm sorry, but are you John Hope Franklin?"

"Please call me John Hope," he said.

"My, my middle name's the same as yours." I felt a wave of embarrassment flood my cheeks. How did I let that slip out?! I looked up carefully to see that he was not offended. To my surprise, he was smiling.

"Ah, yes. I believe your parents named you after me. And I, in turn, was named after my father's mentor in college, a Mr. John Hope." He then went on to reminisce about his father and his education.

"But Mr. Parker," he said, coming to a stop. "I'm not here to tell you about my life. I'm here to talk about yours.

"I heard you decided to speed up our country's acquisition of historical knowledge today. I have to say, I'm proud of what you did, although I don't think I'd ever have the idea of using spray paint. You see, Mr. Parker, my spray paint in life has been my words. Whether spoken or in written form, I made sure my point was clear and strong and understood by all. I think that you, young man, have that same power. You can put pen to paper and show the world what you need them to see."

"But sir—I've already been suspended once and right now I'm sitting in a jail cell," I protested. "How can I make people take me seriously now?"

"Kendrick, do you know many change agents who didn't spend time in jail? You have shown yourself to be a very resourceful person who lives outside the box. I think you can make people take you seriously quite easily. You just need to be yourself and show people who you are and that you are serious about what you do in life," said John Hope, walking past the desks to stand in front of the poster with Lia's name on it. "I'm sure you've noticed these posters are for people in *your* life. Written on them is information about what has not yet happened to them. But, it *will* happen if you show the world who you are and if you help the people you are close to become who they wish to be."

"How can you be so sure this will happen if I'm not even sure who I am?" I once again protested.

"Oh Kendrick, I'm sure you can figure that out pretty easily," said John Hope. He turned away from me and walked to the computer next to the whiteboard. He typed something into it.

In a flash of light, the projector turned on and displayed on the whiteboard a photograph of everyone important to me in my life. There, in the front row were my parents with their arms around each other and Lia right next to them.

"These people depend on you to make the right choices," said John Hope. "I think if you keep that in mind along with the thought that they, too, are trying to be themselves, then you will be able to do what you want in life."

The sound of a rattling lock cut through the pristine air in the classroom.

"Did you hear that?" I asked, startled.

"No, I didn't, which most likely means it's happening on your end of things," said John Hope. "You should be waking up any moment now."

Indeed, I felt the ground underneath me begin to dissolve and I could no longer see details in the room.

"John Hope, before you go, I just heard you died—I'm really sorry," I said.

"Don't be," said John Hope. "Death is not a bad thing. Simply think of it as if my can of spray paint has run out. Goodbye, Mr. Parker."

"Good—" I started to say, but as I reached 'bye,' my eyes opened and a guard was at my cell door.

"Bye," I whispered.

## 24

"Let's go," said a deep voice.

I had been in the cell for what seemed to be days, but was merely hours. It smelled like body odor and burned my nose. I looked up to see who it was when the voice spoke again.

"Get up and follow me."

I rose slowly and cautiously walked toward the open cell door. When we stepped out, I realized the voice came from the same police officer that had arrested me. "Follow me," said the officer as he began to walk down the hall.

As I tagged along after the officer, I looked at the other cells and saw other black teens around my age. Some looked like they could have been my friends. Others were so scary-looking I would have crossed the street if they were coming toward me. But almost all the prisoners were black.

When I began to slow down, the officer barked for me to keep up. As we drew closer to a door at the end of the hall, I was able to make out two figures standing outside the door. One looked like he was signing stacks of papers. The other, shorter one looked around, distraught.

As we stepped through the door, Lia rushed forward and embraced me. "I was so worried about you!" she exclaimed.

"Oh, well, I'm alright," I said as I watched my dad fill out the paperwork.

Walking out of the police department, I looked around and noticed someone was missing. "I asked Shawn if he could drive back early to check on the house while I was getting you out," my father explained. "And before I forget, here's your wallet, Kendrick."

"Thanks, Dad." We all squeezed into his BMW and sat quietly in the car until Dad spoke up. "Well, it's late. You hungry, son?"

"Yeah, I'm starving."

The long drive from the jail back down to the city seemed endless, but I relished every moment: looking out the window at the light of the world, watching the sun dip lower in the sky, admiring my father's tightly-knotted tie. We pulled in to an unexpected treat: Waffle House.

Lia walked ahead, leading the way to golden goodness, as my dad and I strolled cautiously over to the no-longer-yellow building with salt-stained windows. "Isn't it a bit weird we are going to eat waffles at six p.m.?" called Lia as she opened the door.

"Anytime is waffle time!" I called back, earning a groan from my dad. We heard the sound of a broken bell as we walked through the door.

"Welcome to Waffle House, darlin'!" the cheerful cashier greeted Lia and then looked over at us. "And guests!" We looked around for a booth in the diner. I slipped into the inside seat with Lia across from me. Her eyes didn't look directly at me, as if she was trying to avoid my gaze. I don't blame her. I'm a so-called "criminal" in the eyes of the government.

The waitress approached our table. "Good evening. I'm Jo and I will serve y'all today. What would y'all like to drink?" Jo wrote down Lia's and my sweet tea order and my dad's coffee. She dropped two straws on the table and walked away. I fiddled with the straw's wrapper and waited for Jo to bring our drinks.

"So, how's this weather?" I asked awkwardly.

I heard a chuckle come out of Lia. "I guess it's fabulous." I smiled at her response, but I never answered back since our drinks arrived at our table.

"Have y'all decided what y'all want?" Jo asked, raising her left eyebrow. I felt a bit uncomfortable, but then my stomach erupted into the sounds of Dory's impersonation of whale calls. "I would like two waffles, and would you be able to just put a piece of grilled chicken right on top of the stack?" I asked, earning a weird glance from Jo. Lia asked for chocolate chip waffles, and my dad a BLT, which wasn't surprising at all.

"You know," said Lia, "you promised me we would go to the beach today."

"Dad," I said, "would you mind terribly if we headed to the beach for a while before going home?"

"Sure thing," said my dad. "I could use some unwinding, too."

## 25

"It's like I don't even know who I am anymore," I admitted as I dug my bare feet into the sand. The sun had set behind us and turned the whole sky a deepening pink framed with purple. The wind left the taste of salt on my lips, which I now licked nervously. "I go from getting all my clothes from hyped-up, trendsetting stores at the mall to Men's Warehouse," I said solemnly. "I thought this—this get-up, this act was me, and that I had finally found myself, but now I'm just as lost as ever."

"I totally agree with you being lost," she laughed. "Just look at you. You're wearing a suit at a beach," she joked. She was right. Who does wear a suit to the beach? It didn't seem like me. Day by day I was becoming the one person I promised I wouldn't become: someone overly concerned with how others perceived them—this wasn't double-consciousness, it was over-consciousness. I was slowly morphing into a self-conscious Oliver. But wait, aren't people supposed to become their parents?

With that thought, I paused to watch my dad strolling barefoot down the beach. I don't think I'd ever seen him barefoot before. This is not the same father as three months ago. But then again, I was not the same Kendrick as three days ago. I gave Lia a late laugh to her previous remark about my suit that would have made any other conversation awkward, but this conversation seemed to keep its sanity. I looked out into the ocean. Inhaling the warm air, I smelled the slight scent of brine. The moon was just appearing against the now swiftly darkening sky, and the waters reflected the few flecks of gold overhead.

It's like I don't even know who I am anymore.

I turned to Lia. The wind was tossing her curls slightly like the tendrils of some exotic mermaid I had always known, but never really seen for the curiosity she was. The fading sun sculpted her face just right, in light and shadow, to the point where her skin was glistening like she, too, had just emerged from the sea. It was hard to resist staring. I felt a hand touch mine awkwardly.

"Sorry," I said, lamely scratching the back of my hand. Now Lia was playing with her hands, too. It was sort of like we both had something to say but didn't know how to say it. Lia, always the bravest of our pair, opened her mouth first.

"You know, Kendrick I've always liked—"

A car horn beeped, signaling it was time to go.

Lia leaned in to give me what I thought was heading toward a kiss on the cheek, but at that moment Dad honked again. I realized it was time to return to my old life.

"I'll race you to the car!" Lia giggled, starting to run. But before she could go, I grabbed her hand. I don't know what came over me to do that. Lia smiled and finished what she started. She kissed me on the cheek and headed to the car. With a warm feeling left on my face, I swiped off my glasses and wiggled off my tie, which I held up in the air before letting the rising wind carry it out to sea.

# # #

Within the first thirty minutes of the car ride, I was asleep. I woke only as the car pulled into our driveway and discovered Lia's head resting on my shoulder. I climbed stiffly out of the car and groggily said goodbye to Lia as she ambled across the street to her house. My dad was hauling everything from the trunk inside.

Still in a daze, I followed dad into our house and headed upstairs to lie down. As I prepared to collapse, I found a note on the bed:

"History, despite its wrenching pain,
    Cannot be unlived, but if faced
    With courage, need not be lived again.

Lift up your eyes upon
This day breaking for you.
. . .
And say simply
Very simply
With _hope_
Good morning."

A few words from Maya Angelou especially for my young man.
Historians _are_ the conscience of the nation, and you are mine.
I love you, Kendrick Hope.

xo

Mom

## 26

I n the days after we got home from Wilmington, I put away my collared white shirts and skinny black ties (except for the one I had thrown in the ocean), and pulled out some of my favorite clothes from a fondly remembered 'before everything' Kendrick.

A week or two afterward, I had to go to my annual checkup appointment at the doctor's. All was well until it came time for the eye check. I could only read the first four lines of the eye chart, and even those not very well.

So, a week later I was sitting in that weird eye doctor chair with an optometrist standing above me, dilating my eyes. The results showed that my growth spurt the summer before had messed my eyes up and I would now need to wear glasses.

When I saw the selection of frames I could choose from, I couldn't help but crack into a grin. There was a large assortment of Ray Bans, just the type that Malcolm X was famous for. Just the type my dad was famous for. Just the type, in fact, that I had recently stowed away above the refrigerator after carefully popping the lenses back in. After a good ten minutes of comparing looks, I finally decided on a simple black plastic pair.

The day after I got my glasses, I stayed after school to meet with Mr. Douglass to talk about my newest idea for teaching the human race about the Wilmington Massacre.

"Okay, Mr. D., what do you think of this? Design a unit plan that can be taught to eighth graders by anyone. *And*, once we design it, I can go back to my old middle school and test it on them."

I tilted my chair onto its back legs, looking at my teacher expectantly. We were sitting in two of the front row seats, turned in our chairs to face each other. Mr. Douglass was looking off at the posters on his walls, nodding his head.

"You know, Kendrick, I think that just might work. And I have to say, I like the classroom setting for teaching a whole lot better than spray painting streets," he said with a grin.

I had to laugh. "Yeah, I don't think I want to make a habit of getting arrested."

"And you know, Kendrick, this will take a lot of work and research on your part."

"Absolutely, Mr. Douglass. My dad's taking me over to the library at Duke this afternoon to check out some books about the Massacre."

"Alright, Mr. Parker, if you do your part, I'll do mine and look into what it takes to put something into the statewide curriculum."

I smiled, thinking of another man, not so much different from this one, who had called me 'Mr. Parker.'

"Thank you so much, Mr. D.," I said, my thoughts already a mile away on the presentation I would soon begin.

# # #

I spent much of the following months in and out of the library, fact checking and double-checking and meeting regularly with Mr. Douglass to compare our progress. We were hoping I'd be able to test my presentation on an eighth grade class the following fall.

- 27 -

"Kendrick! Come on downstairs, we're going to be late!" my dad called. We were going to go meet with Dr. June Atkinson, Superintendent of Public Instruction for North Carolina. For this occasion, I had felt a need to go back into my black separatist phase and had dressed in a skinny black tie, collared white shirt, and a suit. My glasses were halfway down the bridge of my nose, as always.

The meeting with Dr. Atkinson, who turned out to have short blonde hair and an expression worn only by those who had spent years disciplining wayward students, lasted ninety minutes.

But, in the end, she approved our request to move forward with the curriculum—as a pilot program. Moreover, after discussing the ins and outs of my run-in with some cans of spray paint in Wilmington, we eventually got on to the subject of discipline in general. When I told her about the butter knife incident at the beginning of the year, she was incredulous and decided then and there to have the suspension permanently removed from my record. (I guess that's something you can do when you're superintendent!) When she said those words, I felt as if I could jump out the window and soar out into the air with the flock of pigeons I had watched all morning. I was free! And never, ever again would I let myself be caged.

Dr. Atkinson added, "I understand you are a big fan of John Hope Franklin and his work. I also thought the world of him. Good luck to you in your studies. I look forward to seeing the development of your program."

# # #

In the weeks after the meeting and into the beginning of May, life was pretty uneventful.

Well, mostly uneventful. I *was* featured on the front page of *The News and Observer* as the "Tar Heel of the Week." It seemed everyone was a John Hope Franklin fan, and they wanted to talk to me about his work.

Things with my mom and dad had started to settle down. My mom rented a house a couple of blocks behind ours and I spent my days running back and forth between the two.

I passed all my classes with flying colors and felt pretty good about finals. Well, I guess as good as you can feel about finals, which isn't all that good.

My end-of-year grade in Honors World History was a 100. All that extra research on Wilmington 1898 had really made the difference.

Then, sometime at the very end of May, as I was leaving Mr. Douglass' class, he stopped me at the door and said he wanted to talk to me after seventh period. I went through the rest of the day not really paying attention to anyone. I was concentrating on trying to figure out what he wanted to talk to me about. Was it about the eighth grade curriculum? Did it not work? Had Dr. Atkinson gotten cold feet? Had all the research gone to waste?

Finally, the bell rang at the end of seventh period. I slipped through the hallways, dodging crowds of seniors clustered around their lockers.

I entered Mr. D.'s classroom as a few stragglers from his seventh period packed their bags.

"Ah, Kendrick," said Mr. Douglass looking up from some papers he was reading at his desk. "Come on over here."

As I walked over, he pulled out a drawer on the side of the desk and shuffled through some brightly colored files.

"Here it is," he said, holding out a white piece of cardstock, about twice the size of a note card. I took it and turned it over. Written on it, in fancy

silver calligraphy, were the words "John Hope and Aurelia Franklin's Celebration of Life. June 11, from 3 to 6:30 p.m. Join us in celebrating their lives."

"What's this?" I asked. "Is this for me?"

Mr. Douglass smiled at my confusion. "Yes, Kendrick. I felt that John
Hope would have wanted you to come. So I asked one of his colleagues to
include you and your parents on the invitation list. I hope to see you there."

– 28 –

The Thursday after school got out I woke early and dressed in my very best clothes. I pulled out the tie and white shirt and borrowed a suit jacket from Dad.

Later that afternoon, my mom pulled up in front of the house. She was wearing a dark purple dress I didn't recognize. I caught Dad frowning at it.

We drove to West Campus and parked in the circle in front of the Duke Chapel, which had been specially reserved for the people attending the Celebration of Life—not a funeral, a celebration.

As I entered the towering structure, my eyes felt blinded by the abrupt contrast between the bright sunny day outside and the dark nave. It suddenly felt ten degrees cooler and darkness left me seeing spots for a while. But as my eyes adjusted, I saw how big the place really was. There were dozens of pews. Looking up, the light poured down in diffused colors across the growing sea of people. The organ's enormous pipes bellowed out beautiful music, but it didn't overpower our voices. There were large gold crosses and a ceiling that never ended.

A number of people seemed to recognize me. Maybe from the TV coverage or the piece in the *News and Observer*? I felt my cheeks turn red, but gradually, I grew less embarrassed. A few people came up to me, introduced themselves, and said how impressed they were with my courage and intellect. My parents were so proud of me, almost as proud as Mr. Douglass. I spotted him standing a couple feet away from the crowd with the widest smile I had ever seen pinned to his face.

I walked over to Mr. Douglass and let out the words I didn't get to tell him before. "Mr. Douglass—" I started.

"Don't worry about it, Kendrick." He reached up to squeeze my shoulder. "All I did was direct your sail. You steered the ship."

I spied Lia on the other side of the aisle. She was wearing a bright blue, button-down shirt with her signature acid-washed blue jeans. But today, she also wore a black blazer and one of my skinny ties. How she got it I didn't know. I waited until I thought she saw me, then waved and smiled and waved until she finally noticed and waved back.

The crowd soon settled down and we found seats in the pews. Listening to the speakers, I was amazed at how personally each and every one of them had known John Hope. I marveled at the cast of characters before me. There was Bill Clinton, known to all by his shock of silver hair and starched white collar as the forty-second President; and Vernon Jordan, attorney and long-time friend of John Hope. The people speaking about this renowned scholar had known him at such different periods of his life. There were childhood friends, family members, and professors from all the different colleges he had been a part of.

The speeches were interspersed with music. The Fisk Jubilee Singers performed and I couldn't help but squirm a little as their singing sent a shiver from the back of my collar down to my tightly-laced toes.

After the Celebration, we walked slowly down the steps of the Chapel. I turned around when I reached the bottom of the second set of steps. I stepped as far backward as I could 'til my heels hung over the curb into the street. With my head tilted all the way back so my collar crumpled into my neck, I could see the very tip of the Chapel's spire. I dropped my head back down and stared at the people spilling out from behind the giant doors. I imagined the doors smashing closed and what a glorious sound it would make.

There was a gap in the river of people and the doors did close for a few moments. The next couple of people to come out looked oddly familiar. I squinted my eyes. *Wait—is that Oliver in the suit and tie and, at his arm, Kelsey?* She wore a shimmery dark blue dress that looked as if it had absorbed all its color from the Duke students in Krzyzewskiville. It was the type of dress that would have taken my breath away if I'd seen her in it a month ago. But, times had changed, hadn't they? As the pair of them stepped onto the stone sidewalk, they caught sight of me. They both smiled and waved. I guess Kelsey's old Durham family connections had secured them an invitation.

I turned back around and spotted Mom and Dad standing by the car. I walked up to them.

"You alright, Kendrick?"

"Yes, Mom. I'm alright. Much better than alright."

EPILOGUE

stepped on the school courtyard, smiling in anticipation of what I had planned for today. It was good being a sophomore. Wading through the crowded halls, I made it to Mr. Douglass' class, pausing every other step, saying "hey" to all my friends. As I entered the empty classroom where Mr. Douglass taught, I noticed his brief case wasn't there yet. Knowing I had time to go to my locker, I left to gather my materials.

At my locker, where Lia stood waiting with a huge grin. I smiled at her. "Hey, Lia," I said as I gave her a big hug. She hugged me right back. "You know what today is?" I asked, as I rolled through my combination. She knew exactly what day it was, but she looked at me with a confused face.

"Um, is it your birthday?" she joked as my locker opened.

I sighed dramatically. "Nooo. Today is my sample lesson with the eighth graders, duh." She feigned remembering and then having a eureka moment, her index finger outstretched and her head cocked to the side. I face-palmed myself. "I was using sarcasm, Lia."

She countered, "Hmmm, could you spell that for me?"

I laughed. I grabbed my books and slammed my locker shut.

Jogging over to Mr. Douglass, who was just entering his classroom, I greeted him. "Good mornin' Mr. D! Are the eighth graders from Brogden Middle School still coming?"

Mr. Douglass chuckled. "Actually, we are going to them. So, let's go," he said, steering us down the hall.

We drove up Duke Street toward my old school, my lesson plan on my lap. "Did you start that new project?" beamed Mr. Douglass.

I nodded quickly. "Trust me, it's going very well."

We pulled into Leon Street, slowly making our way to the parking lot of the familiar building. As I got out of the vehicle, I felt confident in what I was about to teach. When Mr. Douglass and I entered the school, the main office was buzzing with phone calls and some students were checking in late.

A tall, young, and meticulously dressed African-American man emerged from a back office and walked over to us. As we shook hands, he said, "Welcome back to Brogden. I'm Andre Jefferson, the new principal. I appreciate what you are doing, Kendrick. Our eighth graders on the Blazer's team are looking forward to your visit." He then walked us in the direction of the class.

The uneven green tiles and white walls were covered in anti-bullying posters and still looked the same. I smiled at the memories. Two years seemed forever ago. And now everything looked so much smaller than it had when I wasn't a giant.

We stopped in front of the classroom. "Kendrick, if you are cool with doing the lesson yourself, I would like to borrow Mr. Douglass," Mr. Jefferson suggested.

"I got it," I said and opened the door. All the students turned to me.

"Good morning," I said. A few students greeted me back and others just sat there with bored expressions. I quickly sized up this very interesting class. A girl was picking at her eyes, darkened with black eyeliner. She was working hard on her rebel status, with her hair clipped behind a skull bow and her leather jacket zipped to the top. There was a guy who looked as if he was an athlete, all built, but he was deep in a book with a number two pencil behind his ear. In front of him was a group of girls wearing matching Brogden Cheerleader sweatshirts and flirting with a group of guys who had on football athletic wear. There was even a girl with bright red hair like Ariel from The Little Mermaid. She was wearing black framed glasses, and freckles scattered over her face evenly. She wore a necklace made of soda can tabs, ignoring everyone, engrossed in reading *The Outsiders*.

I continued to walk up to the teacher, who just happened to my former Social Studies teacher, Mr. Grifton.

"Good to see you, Kendrick!" he said and shook my hand. He added, "I have the file you sent me all loaded up on the computer."

"Thanks, you really know how to treat your former students," I said. Then I jumped right in.

"Who here knows what the Wilmington Massacre was about?" I asked, as I pulled up the PowerPoint I worked on. I saw only one hand go up, "Yes, young lady?" I called on the girl sitting in the way back wearing an oversized sweatshirt with bushy hair struggling to escape her ponytail.

"Was it about the 1998 massacre or something like that?" she asked quietly.

I grinned, clicking to the next slide. "Close. In 1898, Wilmington was the largest and richest city in North Carolina . . ." I watched as some kids soaked up the information like sponges and only the group of flirts sat there uninterested. "But that was before the power grab."

Going on with the presentation, I pulled up the last slide. "As a result of the massacre, Wilmington went into a nose dive. Businesses relocated within North Carolina, many settling in Durham. Some of the founders of North Carolina Mutual, the life insurance company for blacks that was part of Durham's Black Wall Street, were refugees from Wilmington. Their loss, our gain."

I took a breath. "Any questions?" Many hands went up, which made me confident in my presentation. I called on a boy in the front row.

"How did Alexander Manly escape?"

I grinned at his curiosity. "Manly was light-complexioned, which helped him pass as white. The Red Shirts gave him a gun, telling him to shoot Alexander Manly if he saw him." Most of the students laughed, saying things about Alexander Manly shooting himself. I remembered that moment on our walking tour, and how my own nervous laugh should have given my plans away. I then called on a girl with a 'Battle of the Books' shirt who sat in the second row.

She asked, "What made you choose to work on this lesson?"

I leaned on the whiteboard thinking about this question and how to respond to it. I could have said, 'I felt like I needed to make a difference and my role model, John Hope Franklin, gave me inspiration.' It was true, but could they really relate? I looked over to see all students with their eyes on me.

I said, "Does anything ever really piss you off? The food in the cafeteria? How your parents treat you? The lack of open soccer fields in Durham? Well, I was doubly pissed off learning about what happened in Wilmington, and then discovering it has been swept under the rug. We're taught North Carolina history for two whole years and there's not one mention of it!"

I continued, "I was lucky to have two incredible mentors, one in person and the other in a book. I hope all of you get to have Mr. Douglass if you go to Pauli Murray. He is an amazing teacher and encouraged us to ask lots of questions and then dig for our own answers.

"The great historian, John Hope Franklin, also inspired me. I only met him once, in a bookstore. But I read his autobiography, saw how he took a proactive role to fix how history was taught, particularly making sure people of color were included." Holding up a book, I continued, "And his autobiography is available in comic book form." The students laughed at that, as I handed it to a girl in the front row to pass around.

I saw from the corner of my eye a boy wearing thick-framed glasses and with curly dark brown hair cautiously raising his hand. I pointed to him, "Do you have a question?"

He nodded and in a curious, but serious tone, asked, "Are you working on a new project?"

"Well since you asked, yes, I am working on something else. It's also focusing on people forgotten in history." I opened up another folder from my flash drive labeled 'Book-Draft Project.' "It's a historical fiction novel that I'm working on with a friend. It's set during the Civil War, but from the point of view of four teenagers who remain at home, not on the battlefields. One is African American in New Bern, another is a Cherokee whose people sided with the South, another is Lumbee fighting against the Confederacy, and the last is from a girl in a poor white family in Salisbury during the bread riots." I showed them how much I had gotten done, scrolling through my twenty-four pages and running. "This is the sneak peek." I looked over to Mr. Grifton at his desk, who nodded at me to indicate that my time was up. "Thank you for listening." They gave me some generous applause and I floated out the door and headed to the principal's office.

As I was passing the elective classrooms, I met up with Mr. Douglass and Principal Jefferson, who were both talking and smiling. "How did it go?" asked Principal Jefferson.

I smiled. "I thought it went well. No one fell asleep!" I couldn't help but feel successful about it.

"Wonderful, Kendrick! We are discussing how to add this to the eighth grade Social Studies workbook," said Mr. Douglass pointing at the paperwork Principal Jefferson held in his hands.

After saying goodbye to the principal, we drove back to Pauli Murray High. I thanked Mr. Douglass for setting up the visit and walked back to my locker. Lia was standing there with a cheeky smile. "How'd it go, Professor Parker?" she mocked.

I entered my combination as I answered, "Horrible. I got kicked out for inciting a riot." I turned to face her. Her eyes were wide open. "I'm kidding, it went well!" She punched my shoulder again.

"Don't scare me! I'm going to the library, you coming?" she asked. I nodded and collected my supplies, dumping them into my bag. "Don't forget your laptop!" Lia called as she walked away.

I ran after Lia to catch up. Together we walked to the library, passing busy streets and the skate park. "Yo, Ken and Lia!" hollered Shawn as he did a 360. We waved, but kept walking. We made it past the buildings and little shops.

Finally reaching the library, we checked in with the front desk. "Good evening my young scholars," greeted the librarian Jules. We walked over to the biography section, sitting at our regular table. "So, what's the goal for today?" Lia asked curiously looking at my laptop screen.

I opened the folder with the writing and smiled. "We're going to change a little bit more of the way history is taught."

AUTHOR'S NOTE

The history, geography and people of this book may or may not be representative of real people in Durham, North Carolina. We spent days trekking through downtown, observing in the public library, touring the executive offices of North Carolina Mutual Insurance Company, hanging out at the skate park and visiting homes in Kendrick's neighborhood, Trinity Park but we also used our imaginations. However, the story of what happened in Wilmington in 1898 is historically accurate.

We were very fortunate to have many people in the Durham area who knew John Hope Franklin and were willing to share their stories. These included his son, John Whitt Franklin, Duke colleague Professor Ray Gavin, and former student Loren Schweninger. We proudly wore our JHF t-shirts and hoodies around town, and were frequently stopped by people who had a John Hope story to tell.

The Duke Libraries and archives staff was a significant help. They hosted our meetings there and shared from their treasure trove of JHF documents. John Gartrell, the current director of the John Hope Franklin Research Center for African and African American History and Culture, was very patient in providing many cartons of source materials for us to examine.

I want to convey my deep appreciation to the following people who contributed to the making of this Young Adult book. Mystery writer Katie Munger joined us at a critical moment during our writing retreat to be our first critic as we struggled to balance all the possible plots. The author of *Crow*, Barbara Wright, joined us for dinner and helped give us confidence that we could write our own book about Wilmington 1898 to right the historical wrongs.

Over the summer we read the non-fiction work *Claudette Colvin: Twice Toward Justice* as a model for what we hoped to do. Besides being well written (and a National Book Award winner), the book resurrected the story of the "first" Rosa Parks. Fortunately, we were able to get the author, Phillip Hoose, to fly down from Portland, Maine, to speak to the writing of the Colvin story and to offer us feedback on our book outline.

Writing instructor Zelda Lockhart facilitated a working session one Saturday, helping us outline the components of the book. Toward the end of the year, we were joined by historical fiction writer, Sharon Ewell Foster. She read an early draft of the book and provided invaluable advice, which included moving up another scene to the beginning as well as addressing some difficult race issues.

We met with John Hope's editor, Thomas LeBien, now a Vice President at Simon & Schuster, on a visit to Duke. He was a wonderful listener and provided suggestions for the book and insights into the publishing business.

After Young Scholar Izzy Salazar's suggestion of the hybrid graphic approach, I contacted John Hope's son, John Whit Franklin, to see what he thought of the idea. To my delight, he loved it, citing the just published graphic autobiography by Congressman John Lewis. We then invited local artist Jamal Walton, to give a demonstration of how the first excerpt from John Hope Franklin's autobiography could be converted. We were so impressed we hired Jamal, and his colleagues Malcolm Goff and Delvecchio Faison, to do the illustrations.

Just as we were looking for more feedback on the project, Katie Spencer of the Museum of Durham History offered us exhibit space downtown to showcase the project. We jumped at the chance and reconstructed our life size characters out of plywood, assembled a timeline of John Hope's life, and laid out plot elements for visitors to shift around and comment on.

We tried hard to incorporate Durham history into the book. Barbara Blue suggested Kendrick's father might have worked at NC Mutual. We loved the idea and a team went to their downtown corporate headquarters, thanks to a warm welcome by Vice President of Operations, Grace Johnson. We then borrowed her office, the conference room, and the picture with candidate Obama for the book.

The backbone for the project was the planning team. Doug(lass) Coleman is a teacher and mentor, who speaks fluent teenager in most of the cultural dialects. Barbara Blue has packed a lot into her eighty-some years including being a principal and amateur historian. LeRae Umfleet has been our content expert and guide to a lot of the historical resources in the community. Her commitment to getting out the truth about Wilmington 1898 has been a guiding light for this effort. Duke student Katie Fernelius was an energetic session leader and helped with family experience describing how teenagers could get in trouble . . . and the consequences!

Alexa Garvoille, an English teacher from the Durham School of the Arts, was our anchor, coach, and publishing inspiration. She had already collaborated with groups of ninth grade students in publishing their memoir collections. After the entire group of Young Scholars had written the guts of the book, she set out with a smaller team of Scholars to help draw the pieces together. They did everything from ensuring consistency in the point of view to assisting with transitions to writing new sections as needed. Here she is pictured at the Celebrity Dairy Goat Farm with part of her team during a writing retreat: Arthur Harrell, Zakar Campbell, Maritza

Mercado, Eden Segbefia, Izzy Salazar, Layla Mussawir, together with Izzy's mom (and planning team member Sarah Meyer, not pictured) and me. Two more scholars, Zoe Tallmadge and Khari Talley, helped immensely in the final drafts of the novel.

As the dust settled on the bulk of the writing and editing, I took the book file and my trusty iMac to a residency at the beautiful Wildacres Retreat in Little Switzerland to do a final edit. I was so confident in the Young Scholars' skills, I proposed the residency last January when we were still cutting our teeth on the book, and I was selected from among 270 residency proposals. So in a log cabin perched on the side of the hill, I did the fine-tune editing, tightened the connections between Kendrick's and John Hope's sections, and filled in a couple of small sections missed by the students. I kept John Hope foremost in my mind and tried to channel his determination, fervor at bringing history alive, and passion into the book. And the Wildacres staff and other residence artists kept me well fed, laughing, and engaged. The mile-long hikes up to the main retreat center on the mountaintop for each meal also kept the blood flowing to my brain.

Books don't magically appear in print without financial resources. We are very grateful for the additional financial support from Dr. Phail Wynn, Vice President of the Duke Office of Durham and Regional Affairs, and from Dr. Deborah Jakubs, Vice President of Duke Libraries, to illustrate and publish this book.

This was truly a team effort. I observed with joy the evolution during the course of the year of this idea's transformation into a published book. We hope it does John Hope Franklin the justice he deserves.

David Stein
John Hope Franklin Young Scholars Program Director
Durham, NC
October 2014

ABOUT THE AUTHORS

The John Hope Franklin Young Scholars were born on August 12, 2011 in Durham, NC. The parents were David Stein, the Duke Durham Neighborhood Partnership Coordinator, Karen Jean Hunt, the Director of the John Hope Franklin Research Collection for African and African American Documentation at the time, and Professor J. Lorand Matory, the Director of the Center for African and African American Research at Duke.

It was an easy birth as everyone loved John Hope Franklin and was delighted to do something in his honor. The baby's benefactor was Duke Provost Peter Lange, who paid for the toddler's pre-school years. After seeing the success of the group in original research on plantation building technology, the Great Migration, and Freedom Crafters, he provided continuing funding. The National Endowment of the Humanities provided additional funding for the study of Freedom Crafters.

The JHFYS personality changes every year as the rising sixth graders make their mark and the returning Scholars mature each year until they leave "home" in tenth grade. Although the program is in its fifth year, their personality can be described as feisty, creative, smart, and curious.

With the completion of this book, the Young Scholars are creating a documentary on the NC Home Front during the Civil War. They jumped into this study with an encouraging push from our longtime mentor, LeRae Umfleet of the NC Department of Cultural Resources, who also costumed the group in period clothing, taught everyone about medicine during the period, and put the history in context. Watch for the documentary in Summer 2015!

ABOUT THE ILLUSTRATORS

DELVECCHIO FAISON is a local-based artist living in Durham and originally from Clinton, North Carolina. He was inspired to draw when he used to see his ex-stepfather draw his mother at the age of five. Faison's confidence in getting his work displayed increased after working with the well-known Raleigh artist Eric McRay in his studio at Artspace. Faison is currently teaching Visual Art at Lakewood Montessori Middle School and is an adjunct instructor at Durham Technical Community College. His website is artextraordinaire.wordpress.com or facebook.com/artextraordinaire

MALCOLM GOFF learned drawing, painting, printmaking, and textile art at an early age from his mother. He earned a degree in Art Education with a concentration in Printmaking and a minor in Black Studies from SUNY New Paltz. Now residing in Durham, he has been an art educator in Durham Public Schools for nearly 20 years. Malcolm Goff's work blends abstraction with social realism and attempts to balance the things that he believes are important in life: justice, peace, and a reverence for humanity. He has had art shows in New Orleans, Atlanta, and NYC. Goff's work is included in corporate and several private collections. More about Malcolm can be found at upanstore.com or malcolmgoff.carbonmade.com

L JAMAL WALTON's first published comic work was the self-published *Welcome to My Madness* in 1995. His first professional comic book credit was *Digital Webbing Presents #7*. He later he worked on the *Masters of the Universe* and the *Teenage Mutant Ninja Turtle* (TMNT) comic books. His creator-owned comic book projects include *Warmageddon*, *Ungoodwise*, and *Captain Evil & Diabla*. More information about L Jamal Walton can be found at ljamalwalton.com.